# HER DOMINANT
# BILLIONAIRE

### LILY HARLEM

Published by Stormy Night Publications and Design, LLC.
www.StormyNightPublications.com

Cover design by Korey Mae Johnson
www.koreymaejohnson.com

Images by 123RF/Andrey Kiselev and 123RF/sirichoke

1st Print Edition. October 2016

ISBN-13: 978-1539375876

ISBN-10: 1539375870

FOR AUDIENCES 18+ ONLY

This book is intended for adults only. Spanking and other sexual activities represented in this book are fantasies only, intended for adults.

# CHAPTER ONE

The knock at her office door made Imogen's heart skitter. She'd been determined to keep fluttery, knee-weakening thoughts well under wraps during this consultation, but best intentions didn't always happen—especially with this particular client.

"Come in," she called, sitting back in her leather chair and setting her features into her most businesslike, professional expression.

Kane was important, yes, but so was she, and last time he'd visited he'd made her feel like a besotted little girl instead of an independent, successful woman in charge of a branch of Coutts bank. Today she'd keep her wits about her and not let herself fall into his hypnotizing dark eyes or be lured under the spell of his husky, sexy voice.

The door opened and Kane Ward stepped into the room. A shard of sunshine streamed across him and he paused for a moment as though allowing it to spotlight his arrival—it seemed even the stars adored him.

"Good afternoon, Mr. Ward," Imogen said, dropping her gaze down his long, lean frame. She told herself she was taking in the exquisite cut of his suit and not wondering what lay beneath it—because that wouldn't be appropriate, would it? Not with a client.

"I told you last time, please, call me Kane." He strode out of the stream of light, across the room, then stopped on the other side of her desk.

Imogen rose and held out her hand. "Kane, good afternoon. I trust you have been well since we last met."

"Very, thank you." He took her hand and squeezed it gently. There was no shake there. He always turned a formal greeting into a soft, intimate gesture.

Imogen responded with a tighter grip. She was coping just fine in a man's world. He didn't have to treat her like a delicate princess, even though she wouldn't mind him hoisting her onto his trusty steed and galloping away to his castle.

*Castle? Steed? Where did that thought come from?*

"And how have you been?" he asked, studying her. "Did you enjoy your trip to Thailand?"

He'd remembered? Imogen struggled not to show her surprise. Their last meeting had been two months ago, just before she'd taken a rare holiday. She didn't always fancy going alone, but had known she was ready for a break or risk burnout. It had done her good. "Yes, it was lovely. Very relaxing."

"And were you suitably pampered on a paradise beach?" He finally released her hand.

"Yes. It was perfect." Imogen smiled and resisted the urge to touch her face, tuck her hair behind her ears, and fiddle with her necklace. A warmth had spread through her. Their conversation last time hadn't just been idle chit-chat. He'd been interested and remembered what she'd had planned in her life.

"I keep meaning to take some time off and get there myself," he said. "Not just Bangkok for business, but to the beaches, see the sights."

"You should. I highly recommend it." She gestured toward the bucket chair on his side of the desk. "Please, take a seat."

He sat, crossed one leg over the other and curled his hands around the ends of the arms. His fingers were big against the brown leather and his fingernails neat and oblong-shaped. He wore a silver Mille Tourbillion watch that peeked from the cuff of his suit jacket—a timekeeping accessory worth double the price of her Chelsea apartment.

But in her line of work, Imogen was no stranger to extreme wealth, and instead she wondered what his hands would feel like running over her body. It wasn't the first occasion thoughts of Kane's hands had drifted through her mind. The skin on his palms wasn't calloused—he didn't exactly partake in manual labor—and she imagined that he'd be very skilled when it came to pleasing a woman. It seemed to her that he was an expert and pretty damn efficient at everything he did; it made no sense that his determination to be the best of the best wouldn't translate into the bedroom as well.

"About those transfers," he said. "I trust it won't be a problem?"

"No, not at all. I saw your financial director's email. It can be done this afternoon. I'll see to it personally."

"Good."

"You didn't really need to take time out of your busy schedule to attend a meeting about this. Personal international banking is all part of our service."

"And a very good service it is too." He smiled.

"I'm glad you think so." Imogen adored his smile. It softened his eyes and changed him from a fierce individual who owned a global empire to a man who was handsome and charming and intriguing and…

"But there is a reason for me coming in." He leaned forward and set his jaw in a determined way.

"Oh?"

"Yes." He settled his gaze on her. "I want more."

Imogen tried to beat down a flush of heat that was rising up her chest to her neck and cheeks. She was prone to blushing, but was determined not to, not now. "More?"

3

"Yes." He stood and snapped down his suit jacket, removing the barest hint of a crease that had folded in the center. "There is something I need to discuss with you, Imogen." He narrowed his eyes and looked down at her. "I can call you that, can't I?"

"Yes. Yes, of course." Anytime. She loved the way he said her name, his English public school accent plumping out the vowels.

"Excellent."

She watched as he walked to the window and studied the London skyline. What on earth could he want from her? From the bank? He had the most privileged and exclusive account available. Mr. Kane Ward was one of Coutts' most valued customers and he had every service at his disposal from one of the most highly regarded financial companies in the world. The bank Her Royal Highness the Queen used.

"It's... delicate," he said, pushing his hands into his suit trouser pockets and standing in yet another bright spot of sunlight. "What I need you to do."

"We can do delicate."

"We?"

"Yes."

"What about you?" He turned. "I said what I need *you* to do."

For a moment Imogen saw him in silhouette—broad shoulders, neat waist, long legs—then he stepped away from the window and up to her desk. He came to stand at her side, bypassing the wide piece of furniture that had been between them and had afforded her protection from the sexy but dark energy he emitted.

"Only you can help, Imogen," he said quietly but with a note of non-negotiation in his tone.

"I'm sure it can be arranged." She paused and cleared her throat. "Whatever it is that's er... delicate and you need me to do."

"I require this transfer within my bank accounts because of a new venture."

"I figured as much." Imogen paused. "But it's all your money, you're not borrowing any, so it's not really Coutts' business what the reason is. You just need to instruct us and we'll do it."

A smile tugged at his mouth. "Much as I like obedience"—he set his backside against Imogen's desk and leaned onto it—"I really would like you to make this your business. Your particular business."

She could smell his cologne. It was woody and thick, a sensual, blatant scent that seemed to invade every cell in her nose and her lungs. "What do you mean?"

"It's new territory. I've, if you'll excuse the expression, had my fingers in many pies, but this…"

"Go on."

One side of his mouth twisted into a half smile. "Well, let's just say this is infiltrating into something more personal." He paused. "Much more personal."

"I don't understand."

"I don't want you to. Not yet anyway." He stood and crossed his arms. His suit tightened around his biceps, highlighting some damn fine muscles that lay beneath.

"Okay." Imogen drew out the last syllable. She didn't say anything else. She'd let him fill the silence even though she felt at a disadvantage being lower than him in her seat.

But it was a silence that stretched on and on. The only sound was the self-important ticking of the grandfather clock in the corner.

He kept his gaze on her.

Imogen swallowed and hoped her cheeks weren't flushing. This was what had happened last time. She'd blushed as he'd stared at her. She hadn't known what to say and thoughts of him—as a man, not as a client—had swirled in her mind, bringing with them images of him naked, of her naked, of them together… naked.

"I'd like to request your company tomorrow," he said eventually, his voice low and grating, as though speaking over sandpaper.

"On official bank business?"

"If that makes it easier for you to take a day out of the office, yes."

"Day out?" That was unheard of. She was a workaholic, barely took time away from her desk to eat and sleep.

"Yes. A day away from all of this." He indicated the wooden paneled walls and the huge window. "A day out with me discussing my new business venture. It is only you, Imogen, who can help, so I really must insist."

"Really?" She was sure he had a hundred minions at his beck and call. "But—?"

"Yes." He tilted his chin and a small muscle twitched beneath the neat layer of beard he sported. "So do you agree?"

"Well, yes, of course. If it's vital."

His mouth tipped into a satisfied smile. He was clearly a man who liked to get what he wanted—every time. "I'll have my driver pick you up at ten."

"From—?"

"Your home in Chelsea."

"You know where I live?" She couldn't keep the astonishment from her voice.

"Naturally. You hold the key to my assets, Imogen White, which means I know everything about you."

Her breath caught in her throat. So he wasn't interested in her for her. It was merely because she had his accounts at her fingertips.

He smirked. "Please don't look so alarmed. I haven't been stalking you. I just like to know the details about my inner circle, and you, Imogen, are definitely in that circle."

Alarm warred with flattery. She was in Kane Ward's inner circle? *The* Kane Ward. Yes, of course she was. She'd been handling his accounts for several years. They'd known each other for just as long, in a professional sense, of course. Why wouldn't she be in his inner circle?

"So ten o'clock," he said. "Wear something pretty, and a hat if you have one."

*Pretty? A hat? What the...?*

"You mean... not a suit." She glanced down at the gray pencil skirt she'd teamed with a matching jacket that morning. Beneath it she wore a simple white silk shirt and a string of red beads that matched her heeled shoes.

"Much as power dressing is very attractive," he said, following her line of sight, "I think you'd be more comfortable in a dress."

"Where are we going?" Imogen beat down a wave of panic. A dress? Bloody hell. Did she have any pretty dresses in her wardrobe? And a hat?

"Ah, that's for me to know and you to find out. But you will enjoy it, I promise." He shoved back the sleeve on his jacket and glanced at his watch. "I have to go."

Imogen stood and pressed her hand over her thighs, pushing the faint lines from her skirt. "Yes, of course, and I'll follow your instructions to the letter and get your accounts switched exactly as you want."

"Perfect." He smiled.

It was a little shady, though, secretive, as if she'd said something in a way that had pleased him over and above his banking business.

She wasn't sure what.

He reached for her hand. She thought he'd shake it in that gentle, intimate way he always did, but instead he drew her knuckles up close to his mouth and hovered his lips just above them.

"Until tomorrow," he said, his breath warming her flesh.

Imogen was aware of a zing of excitement flooding through her and she watched, mesmerized as he kissed her skin.

She opened her mouth. No words came out.

He looked at her from beneath long dark lashes and with his slightly moist lips still on her flesh. His nose had a small bump in it she hadn't noticed before, as though it had maybe been broken a long time ago.

She shut her mouth and held his gaze. It was as if he

were assessing her reaction to his gesture.

She was assessing all right. Kane Ward had kissed her hand. What the hell did that mean?

But was she complaining?

Hell, no.

He straightened and released her.

Imogen dropped her hand to her side and clenched her fists. She wanted to press the patch of skin to her own lips, catch any lingering flavor or scent of him. But she didn't. She wouldn't let him know that she craved finding out more about him, the man. That wouldn't be professional. She'd have to keep that under wraps.

"We'll have a very interesting day," Kane said, stepping toward the door. "I can tell."

• • • • • • •

Imogen stared at her wardrobe. What was she going to do? A wall of trouser and skirt suits faced her, along with a collection of plain blouses, all perfect for wearing with them.

Other than that she had sweats, jeans, and t-shirts that she flung on when home from the office and all she wanted to do was chill out. It seemed she'd bypassed pretty shopping altogether—it just wasn't on her radar. There was nothing pink or flowery or vaguely sweet hiding amongst the block colors and neat lines.

"Bugger." She glanced at the clock. It was past nine. Far too late to nip to King's Road, and there was no way she'd get an internet delivery before ten the next morning even if she did find something she liked online. Which was highly unlikely—she had no idea what kind of *pretty* dress to go for and as for the hat...?

There was only one thing for it. She'd have to go and see her neighbor, Clarris, and root through her cupboard to see if she had anything she could borrow. It was improbable; Clarris was a single mother who worked on Fleet Street. She spent her days in the same kind of clothes as Imogen with the only difference being her casual clothes often had sticky patches on them from her three-year-old daughter, Katie.

Imogen locked up her apartment and went to the next door along her side of the building. She knocked quietly, knowing that Katie would be in bed after a long day with the childminder and Clarris likely relaxing with a glass of wine and the latest episode of *Eastenders*.

"Hey, Imogen. Are you okay?" Clarris asked, pulling open the door, predicted glass of wine in hand and her hair a little squashed on one side, giving the impression she'd been lying on the sofa.

"Yes, well, no. I've got a dilemma."

Clarris raised her eyebrows. "Oh, that sounds interesting."

"It is." Imogen frowned. "Remember that guy I told you about, the handsome client."

"The billionaire customer?" She opened the door fully. "Get in here and tell me all about it." The sleepy quality had left her voice.

"The billionaire, well, yes, but most of them are where I work. The one with the—"

"Hypnotizing eyes and sexy voice." She shut the door and grinned. "Once dated a princess and owns half of London."

"Well, I don't know if they dated, and I think half of London might be an exaggeration. He owns several shops, a couple of restaurants, a hotel, and an upmarket estate agency but—"

"Kane Ward." Clarris held up her glass in triumph. "Number eighteen on the UK's rich list, tops every eligible bachelor list and you've barely touched on what he owns."

"Bloody hell. How do you remember all of this stuff?" Imogen stared at her friend aghast. "I should be more careful what I tell you."

"I remember everything everyone tells me and then I dig for more info, my dear. I'm a journalist, don't you know.

Being nosy is not just my profession, it is also my addiction."

"You're not kidding." Imogen strolled into the living room and spotted a half drunk bottle of pinot grigio. "Can I?"

"As long as it will loosen your tongue. I need details." Clarris reached for a wineglass from the open-plan living area and passed it over. "Juicy gossip."

"You need juicy gossip, I need a dress." Imogen filled the glass halfway then took a slug.

"A dress. What sort of dress?" Clarris sat on the edge of the sofa and leaned forward.

"Something pretty."

"Okay…" She looked thoughtful. "When for?"

"Now, well, not now, tomorrow."

"Why?"

"He's taking me out?"

"Kane Ward?"

"Yes."

"Where?"

"I don't know."

"During the day?"

"Yes."

"And it has to be a dress and it has to be pretty? Why?"

"Yes. Blimey, slow down with the questions." Imogen had another sip of wine.

"Just trying to help." Clarris raised her hands as if in surrender. Her wine sloshed to the side of the glass.

"I haven't got anything," Imogen said with a sigh. "And that's all he said, wear something pretty because I need your advice."

"Your advice?" Clarris said, frowning.

"Yes, a new business venture that only I can help him with. So he said."

"And he wants you to wear something pretty to this meeting?"

"And a hat."

"A hat! What the…?" Clarris set her drink on the table and rubbed her hands together. "This is so exciting. *The* Kane Ward wants you to be dressed all pretty, and in a hat, and is taking you out to discuss a new business venture. Fucking hell, this is the stuff of your wet dreams, girl."

"How would you know?" Imogen frowned.

Clarris gave Imogen a look that said *Don't try to deny it.*

Imogen huffed. Was she really so transparent? "That kind of sums it up, yes, but I'm still no nearer to a pretty dress." She wafted her hand down her body. "All I have is work stuff or casual stuff."

"I wonder why…?" Clarris frowned. "What kind of place would a billionaire take a sexy woman dressed pretty in the middle of the day—?"

"Well, I don't know if he thinks I'm sexy, it's just business."

"Oh, shut up. Have you stood in front of a mirror lately?"

"I—"

"You're bloody gorgeous and he's damn lucky to be taking you out. Successful, independent, and single. Single because you never have time to date."

Imogen felt arguments stacking up on her tongue. She didn't date because no one had taken her fancy. If someone had, she'd have time, she'd make the time.

"And if you ask me," Clarris continued quickly. "Kane Ward is a brilliantly smart man tricking you into going on a date by telling you it's business. Seems to me that's the surest way to get you to say yes."

"It *is* business." Imogen frowned.

Clarris stood, set down her wine, put her hands on her hips. "Oh, no, this isn't business, this is horse racing."

"What?"

"It's June and that means one thing, the sport of kings."

"You're talking in riddles."

"It's Royal Ascot this week and tomorrow is Ladies' Day. I've sent one of my team to cover it."

"But why would he take me there?" Imogen rubbed her temple. She'd never been to the races in her life. Why on earth would Kane Ward want to take her? "You can't be right."

"Oh, but I am. And the weather forecast is lovely, perfect for a pretty dress and a hat. He's going to spoil you rotten in *the* place to be seen in June."

"Do you really think so?"

"I'd bet Katie's best teddy on it. He's not the sort of man, from what I gather, to take a girl for a pizza or a walk in the park. He'll only do anything if it's the best."

"Fuck."

"Language, you're a lady, remember. Or at least he thinks that." She reached for Imogen's hand. "Come on. I can help. You've come to the right place."

"I have?" Imogen said, thoughts of what tomorrow would entail rushing through her mind. Could Clarris be right? Was Kane taking her to the races? She wouldn't have a clue what to do. Would she be expected to bet? Surely they were just going to lunch somewhere. He'd said he liked power dressing; perhaps he was just living up to his reputation for making demands and having them met by ordering her to wear something different, just to see if she would.

"I'm really not sure about this," Imogen said.

"Of course you are. Come on, I haven't got much. You see me going to work, I'm a black suit kind of gal, and of course this." She gestured at her tatty jeans and frayed sweater. "But I have got that dress I wore to my sister's wedding last year, when I was a bridesmaid. That's pretty, beyond pretty."

"Is it pink?" Imogen's heart sank. She knew it was. She remembered the flowery number. Had seen it in the photographs. She really couldn't imagine wearing anything so girly.

"Behave and stop pouting," Clarris said, standing. "And come this way." She gripped Imogen's hand tighter and whizzed her through to the bedroom.

The place was a tip. Clothes and makeup and hair products everywhere and the bed unmade, the duvet a mountain-like twist in the center. It smelled of perfume and hairspray and fabric conditioner.

"It's in here," Clarris said, letting go of Imogen and kicking a pair of long black patent boots out of the way so she could get to a wardrobe. She pulled out a sheer chiffon dress in the palest pink. Cerise flowers circled the hem then thinned and became smaller as they dissipated toward the waist. It had a slim white belt, and the material became so pale that by the time it rose in scallops over the chest it was nearly white. In fact, the delicate spaghetti straps were white.

It wasn't nearly as over the top as Imogen remembered. "Oh…" she said. "It is pretty." Imogen took it and surveyed it at arm's length. It looked her size; luckily she and Clarris were both roughly the same height and weight.

"Very, my sister was pink crazy but we talked her down from the ledge on this one and compromised." Clarris reached upward to a shelf and grabbed a hatbox.

"This," Clarris said, dumping the box on the bed, "is perfect for Ladies' Day." She pulled out a small but fancy hat. It had pretty loops made of stiff lace set in an intricate bow at an angle, a narrow upturned brim, and was the same shade as the darker flowers on the dress.

Imogen stared at it and her heart beat faster. It wasn't something she had ever thought of wearing, but now she looked at it she suddenly wanted to, desperately. She was going to the races with Kane Ward—a man she'd secretly fantasized about, and in the dead of night touched herself and imagined his hands on her, bringing her release.

None of it she'd thought would actually be in her future. But it seemed it was, and now all she had to do was maintain control and make sure she stayed businesslike and professional at all times. Kane wasn't a man who liked weak or easily manipulated people around him, so she had to show him she wasn't.

# CHAPTER TWO

Imogen had set her alarm clock, her iPhone, and had asked Clarris to call her at seven o'clock, just to be sure she didn't oversleep. As it was, she was awake before any of the alarms went off. She was eager to get on with the day, keen to see if Clarris had been right and a trip to Ascot really was the plan.

"Have fun," Clarris said, when she called.

"I'm sure I will. But it's business, remember, even if it is somewhere lovely."

"Yeah, yeah, you just keep telling yourself that."

"It is."

"Okay, but like I said, have fun, flirt a little. It will do you good."

"What do you mean?"

"To have some male company. *Handsome* male company. And let's face it, you could do a lot worse."

Imogen was quiet. Clarris was, of course, right.

"And if you are at Ascot, Imogen, drop me a text and let me know where, which stand. I can send my rover there to take a paparazzi shot. It will be worth good money, a pic of Kane Ward and his new squeeze."

"Er… no, I won't. Because I'm not his new squeeze."

Imogen shook her head. She was at a loss as to what to say to her incorrigible friend. She didn't know whether to laugh or be cross.

Clarris giggled. "See you later. And if he wants to use his tongue, let him."

"Clarris!"

The phone line went dead. Imogen stared at the receiver. She was hardly going to kiss Kane while they were at a meeting discussing his new business venture. She glanced down at her right hand and stroked over her knuckles. But could she be sure? Yesterday he'd done just that. Lifted her hand to his mouth and brushed his lips over her skin. She could still feel his touch, remembered his warm breath, and the way he'd studied her, as though fascinated by her reaction. That had been—wow, that *look* had been hot. For a moment it had felt like time had stood still, like they were the only two people in the world. For a moment, anything could have happened.

Which was, of course, ridiculous, fanciful thinking. Nothing would have, or was, going to happen.

She checked the time then jumped in the shower. She took extra care shampooing and conditioning, applied a face mask, then ensured not a body hair was out of place.

After drying and applying expensive sweet-smelling body butter, she pulled on white lacy underwear and a pair of sheer hold-up stockings. After drying her hair and creating big, bubbled curls, she pinned them loosely. She kept her makeup minimal, but her lipstick was dramatic and matched the deep pink on the dress.

She ate a slice of toast and drank a cup of tea then realized the time was ticking on. She slipped into the dress, which thankfully fit beautifully, stepped into pale silvery sandals and grabbed a shawl, just in case the weather changed. She added the hat at a jaunty angle and secured it with a pin.

She checked outside. The sky was a rich, deep blue and the sun was forecast to shine unhindered by clouds for the entire day.

A long black car pulling up at the entrance to Bellview Towers caught her attention. She checked the time. It was spot on ten.

Was that Kane? Had he arrived?

Quickly, she applied a squirt of Eternity, scooped up her iPhone and purse, then left the apartment. Her breathing had picked up and she hoped she wouldn't get flushed and sweaty. The last thing she needed were cheeks that looked as though they'd been slapped.

But unfortunately just the thought of Kane Ward outside her building, within yards of her—and her bedroom—was enough to send sexy thoughts spiraling around her mind and had her cheeks tingling. He was here. He really had arrived.

She took the elevator to the ground floor, fiddling with the position of her hat as she studied her reflection in the mirrored doors.

Once in the lobby, she took a deep breath. There really was no need to be nervous. She fit Kane's brief despite the short time frame he'd given her to find a dress, the sun was shining, and all that was required of her was to wear her business manager smile and treat her customer's assets as if they were her own—with respect, consideration, and minimizing risk at all times.

The sun warmed her shoulders as she stepped into the open. She saw that it was no ordinary car but a sleek black limousine complete with top-hatted driver.

The chauffeur, an older man with a smart black mustache, spotted her.

"Ms. White?" he asked.

"Yes." Imogen glanced at the blacked-out windows. Why was she surprised? Of course Kane would have a limo. It went with the territory when a person was as wealthy as he was.

"Mr. Ward is expecting you."

"Oh." She couldn't see into the car. Did that mean he

wasn't in there?

The driver pulled open the rear door, exposing shiny black leather seats and a huge expanse of legroom. No Kane.

"Mr. Ward sends his apologies. An urgent conference call came up and he was delayed. He's waiting for you at our destination."

"That's okay. Business first," Imogen said, smiling the way she would at work, to a client.

"Yes, ma'am." He indicated that she get into the car. "Please, make yourself comfortable."

Imogen climbed in and set her purse on the seat next to her. There was enough room for about eight people in the back of the car, and when the driver shut the door it went dark for a moment, then small lights at feet level illuminated the floor as did several spots in the ceiling.

She crossed her legs and reached for her seatbelt. Once fastened, she held it forward so it didn't crease her dress. She'd been in a limo once before, but it had been years ago. One of her university friends had gotten married and on the hen night they'd all dressed up, drunk cheap sparkling wine, and driven around London for an hour before getting dropped off at Dover Street Bar. It had been fun, but it had been different to this. Now she felt tiny in the big car, as though it had swallowed her up.

She could see the back of the driver's head through a darkened screen. She wondered if Kane ever brought women into the back of this car and kissed them, touched them, whispered dark deeds into their ears.

Imogen skimmed her hand over the cool leather at her side and imagined him sitting there. Imagined that she was one of those women and he was looking at her in that intense way of his. Reaching for her, slipping his hand behind the back of her neck and pulling her close. She could almost taste him, smell him. She wondered what it would be like to be one of those women, a list of names and faces that must surely be endless. He could have his pick of females the world over from A-listers to supermodels to royalty and starlets on the TV.

The driver took the car over Wandsworth Bridge and headed east. She'd never seen Kane Ward officially linked to anyone, though. She'd only heard rumors. His private life was just that, private. Clarris was off her trolley if she thought Imogen would let their location be known so he could get a photo. If indeed it was Ascot they were going to. For all she knew they could be going to a conference center or a hotel meeting room.

As they drove she began to feel less sure about her outfit. She hoped she hadn't dressed ridiculously over the top. Perhaps he'd meant something more casual, a meeting room dress that just wasn't as formal and the whole hat thing might have been his perverse idea of a joke? She glanced down at the dress and traced one of the flowers over her thigh. Well, if that was the case she'd just make the most of it. Take the hat off and hope her hair stayed elegantly up and wrap the shawl around her shoulders. She'd adapt. She had in the past when the need had been called upon.

On and on the driver went, expertly moving around London traffic.

Imogen looked out of the shadowed windows. She didn't often venture toward Battersea. There was nothing there that she could think of in terms of elegant meeting rooms. Maybe the business venture was in this area and they were going straight to the guts of it to have a look around.

But why the dress?

Eventually, the limo slowed and turned into a concrete car park. In the distance, power station towers loomed large, and in front of her, sat on long, sleek skids, was a helicopter. It was black and shiny with a gold stripe running horizontally around it.

The place seemed deserted. No sign of Kane or anyone else.

The car was pulled to a halt. She released her seatbelt. Through the tinted windows she could make out what appeared to be a low building, a reception area maybe. Was Kane thinking of going into the executive helicopter business? If so, she'd highly recommend it. There were plenty of VIPs and celebs that would be glad of vertical routes in and out of the capital. It would be a good investment for sure.

"Ma'am," the driver said, opening the door.

"Thank you," she said, stepping out and breathing in the warm air that was a direct contrast to the air conditioning she'd been sitting in.

"Mr. Ward is waiting." The driver indicated behind her.

Imogen turned.

Standing in the shadows of a perimeter wall was Kane. He had his back to her and was talking on the phone. He was perfectly still, though the low timbre of his voice filtered her way.

Suddenly he turned. His attention settled on her. "I have to go." He slipped his phone into his breast pocket and pushed the center of his shades, sliding them up a little. He stepped from the darkness into the sunlight.

Imogen swallowed as he approached and a wave of shyness washed through her. Damn, the guy was so seriously good-looking he could have just walked off an Armani advert. What the hell was she doing having lusty thoughts about him? He was way out of her league. He may as well be the king of England for all the chance she had with him.

"Imogen," he said, his voice low and husky. "You're here."

She couldn't tell if he was pleased or displeased with the fact she was there. His eyes were hidden behind black lenses and his mouth was a dead straight line. He'd revealed nothing in the way he'd spoken.

"You look," he said, poking out the tip of his tongue and dampening his bottom lip, "exquisite."

Heat prickled between Imogen's breasts and her belly tensed. "Will it be suitable?" She breezed her hand over her waist, smoothing the already flat material.

"It's perfect." He smiled.

A sense of delight went through her at having pleased the great Mr. Ward, but also a feeling of having been captured, like a butterfly in a net. She'd flitted and fussed but had no real chance of escape. He'd known he'd get her to agree to this day.

"Shall we?" he said, gesturing to the helicopter.

"We're going up in that?" she asked, eyeing the blades as they started to turn slowly.

"Yes. I can't bear London traffic. If I can drop in somewhere from the sky, I do."

"Well, yes, good idea." Imogen had never been in a helicopter. It didn't exactly frighten her, but as heights were not her thing she couldn't help a few trepidations.

"You'll be perfectly fine," he said, skimming his hand against her lower back and urging her forward. "She's a state-of-the-art Sikorsky. Peter and Joel have been flying her for over a year now."

Imogen looked at the front window and spotted a pilot wearing a headset. "I'm okay," she said, as much to herself as to Kane.

"Are you sure? I would hate you to do something you didn't want to or weren't comfortable with."

"I'm perfectly fine." She added a little pace to her stride. She didn't want him to think she was a scaredy cat, because she wasn't. She was a strong, independent woman.

"Good." He paused as a pilot dressed in a black suit and peaked cap, like the chauffeur, pulled open a door, revealing the interior.

It was not as Imogen had expected—much more opulent. The four huge seats were wide and made of beige leather. The walls were reddish-colored wood, and between two of the chairs was what appeared to be a bar complete with glasses and optics and a golden K.W. embossed into the wood. A screen hung on the wall and the floor was covered in plush cream carpet.

"Please," Kane said, "come in and make yourself comfortable." He stepped in and held out his hand.

Imogen pressed her hat as the slight breeze from the ambling rotor blades shifted it slightly. She took his hand.

He held her gently but firmly as she climbed up into the helicopter. "It's... big," she said. It was pure decadence. There was enough space for possibly ten seats, yet it had so few and the pilot compartment was screened off.

"It's the best money can buy in this size range."

"I'm sure." She looked at him. "But that's what I would expect from you. The best money can buy." She'd seen enough of his accounts to know that was the way he operated. Everything he owned was the best of the best. He didn't do compromise.

He smiled and indicated one of the forward-facing seats. "Would you like a drink?"

"No. I'm fine. Thank you." Imogen sat. The leather was exquisitely soft and also cool.

Kane sat, crossed his legs, and nodded at the pilot, who was standing sentry-like on the tarmac.

The door was shut.

"So where do you think our destination is today?" he asked, his gaze seeming to slide down her legs and settle on her foot.

She noticed she was bouncing her toe slightly but quickly stopped. "I don't know. You said you wanted to discuss a new business venture. But we can talk anywhere, we could have discussed it yesterday in my office."

"Ah, yes. Your office."

"What about my office?" She turned to him.

"When did you last have a day out of it? And I'm not talking about that trip to Thailand, your first holiday in three years. I mean a Monday to Friday that you weren't there?"

Imogen stared at him. "How did you—?"

"Know? Easy. I wanted the information so I found it."

Imogen tightened her fingers around her purse. "But why would you be interested in how much time I spend in my office?"

"Because…" He leaned forward and settled his attention on her face again. "I'm interested in *you*."

Suddenly the engine roared and Imogen felt the huge machine shift. She released her purse and gripped the arms of the seat. "Bloody hell."

"It's okay," he said, smiling and resting his hand over hers. "It's supposed to do that." He had to raise his voice a little, over the sound of the rotors.

"You sure?" She liked the weight and heat of his hand, but still her stomach lurched.

"Yes." He chuckled. "Maybe I should get you that drink?"

"No, no, I'm fine, really."

The noise increased and Imogen tipped forward as the helicopter took off. She sucked in a breath and bit on her bottom lip.

Kane sat back but kept his hand over hers. He smiled.

"It's okay for you," she said. "This is my first time."

"New experiences are always of benefit to one's soul."

"I suppose." She looked out of the window at the ground shrinking into the distance.

The vehicle leaned to the right and the wide, muddy Thames came into view. They then seemed to follow its meander, heading inland. Imogen studied St. Paul's Cathedral peeking from the rooftops as they flew past. "Wow, that's amazing."

"Great view, don't you think?"

"Yes, it's incredible." Her nerves subsided as the beauty of London, looking so handsome in the sunshine, stunned her. "I love this city," she said. "I always have done and always will." She leaned to see past him and gestured to the London Eye.

"Have you been for a spin?" he asked, finally lifting his hand from hers.

She missed his warm touch. It had been both comforting and sensual. "I haven't had the time. Which is shameful, really."

"You work too hard, that's what I've decided."

"Oh, *you've* decided, have you?" She turned to him. "Do I get an opinion?"

"Of course, but it's unlikely to change mine." A slight frown plowed across his usually smooth brow.

She shook her head. If there was one thing she'd suspected previously about Kane Ward, it was that he was stubborn. Now she was pretty damn sure of her deduction.

"I work hard," she said, "because I owe that to the bank and to the clients."

"But all work and no play could make Imogen a dull girl."

"You think I'm dull?" Her heart sank. She didn't think she was dull, but to a man like Kane, who could do anything, go anywhere, and have whatever he wanted, then she probably was... very.

"On the contrary." He placed the tip of his finger on her first knuckle and traced over the rise of her wrist then slowly up her forearm.

Each tiny section of flesh he touched fizzed and tingled. She held her breath.

"I think you're very interesting, Imogen," he said. "I also value your opinion on all matters, so please don't ever think that I don't."

She slowly let her breath out. "Okay."

That was the second time he'd touched her in a way that was not entirely appropriately for a client to touch his bank manager. Not that she was about to protest. She was just confused. And what about this new business venture?

He lifted his hand from hers and placed it on the arm of his chair.

"Where are we going?" she asked.

"Where do you think?"

"I don't know."

"You must have an idea."

"I suppose."

"And, what is that idea?" He removed his glasses, then slotted them into the inside pocket of his jacket.

"I feel like I'm dressed for the races." Damn, she hoped she hadn't been too presumptuous. What if they were going to some factory to look around, or for a business lunch just out of the city? She stared into his eyes, hoping for a clue now that she could finally see them.

He nodded, slowly. "Clever thing. I knew you'd get it."

"So we are going to Ascot?"

"Of course, it's Ladies' Day. Every gentleman needs a beautiful lady on his arm on Ladies' Day."

Fuck. Did he just call her beautiful? Blood simmered to the surface of her cheeks. It raced there, hot and vital, and before she knew it her face was on fire.

Oh, how she hated being a blusher. It didn't matter how sophisticated she looked or how elegantly she was trying to behave, her skin just pinked up of its own volition. It prickled and itched and felt like fire had been thrown over her. Hell, it wasn't as if she hadn't been called beautiful before—just not by Kane Ward.

Kane raised his eyebrows.

She looked away, out of the window. "How long will it take to get there?"

"Another ten minutes at the most."

"Okay." She'd just have to feign fascination in the passing landscape until her face stopped resembling a beetroot. But he'd seen, she knew he had. Now he'd think she was a silly little girl.

Drat and double drat.

# CHAPTER THREE

Why had she never been to the races before? The atmosphere was electric and the sense of excitement and anticipation seemed to make the air crackle. Imogen loved it instantly.

Once off the helicopter, despite being offered a ride to the hospitality suite, she'd suggested they walk. Imogen wanted to soak up the ambience, catch a glimpse of the horses being shown off in the parade ring, and see the outfits and hats on display.

And wow, what a selection of hats. Hers, although pretty and detailed, was positively plain in comparison to some. Not that she was complaining; she had other things on her mind rather than worrying about giving someone a concussion with her headwear.

She pointed out a particularly large, feathered hat to Kane. It looked like a peacock was sitting on the woman's head. "What do you think?"

"Ridiculous," he said, continuing to stride forward.

Imogen quickened her pace to keep up with him.

"I'm sure it will get her picture in the paper though," he said over his shoulder.

"And she'll no doubt be thrilled."

A man, with a flat cap and *Racing Post* under his arm, bumped shoulders with Kane. It was a heavy connection and Kane shifted to the right.

"Sorry." The man huffed, kept his head down, and didn't pause.

Kane halted and clenched his fists. His body tensed. He stared straight ahead at the swarming crowd.

"You okay?" Imogen asked, drawing level with him.

"We should have taken the ride."

"Oh, I'm sorry. You should have said."

"It's okay. But come on. This way." He took her hand and set off at a brisk pace. His grip was tight and firm.

"I wouldn't have minded catching a ride," she said. "If that's what you would have preferred."

"You wanted to walk. We're walking."

"But—"

"It's okay. I just don't generally have to be near people I don't know, don't employ, or don't want to be around."

Up until a minute ago, Imogen wouldn't have imagined anything could have bothered Kane Ward. But now she knew differently. He really wasn't enjoying milling with the masses. If the air at Ascot was crackling with excitement, he was crackling with discomfort.

Soon they approached a thick white rope stretched between two posts. A race official was guarding it and he held a clipboard against his chest.

Kane strode straight up to him. "Ward," he all but barked.

"Ah, yes, sir. We've been expecting you." The official smiled and unhooked the rope. He hadn't needed to consult his list.

As soon as Kane stepped onto the privileged section of the course—free from touts and gamblers and excited, hatted ladies—his body language changed. His shoulders relaxed, as did his grip on Imogen's hand.

"If you'd like to follow me, sir," the official said, turning.

Kane pulled in a deep breath and smiled at Imogen. He

appeared back to his usual, charming, composed self. "Shall we?" He gestured forward.

"Yes, of course."

Imogen walked in line behind the official, who led them into a red-bricked building, up a staircase then into a large room that had one round table in the center. It was dressed in white linen, set for two, held a silver candelabra and the seats had plush gray cushions on them. Beyond the table were large French doors leading onto a balcony containing several terracotta pots bursting with summer bedding. Like the helicopter, the room appeared to be designed to house many more people than it was prepared for.

"I trust everything is as instructed?" the official said, almost bowing at Kane.

Kane glanced around. His gaze settled on a long, low red velvet sofa that was angled to face the doors. "Perfect."

"Champagne, madam?"

Imogen turned to her right. A young woman, dressed entirely in black and with pale lipstick, held a silver tray. Upon the tray were two flutes of sparkling liquid that had bubbling mist popping over the rims.

"Thank you," Imogen said, taking one.

Kane also helped himself, then slipped his hand to the small of Imogen's back and steered her toward the French doors.

Once outside, Imogen could see that they had a spectacular view of the course. The finish line was directly in front of them, as were, about three stories down, a mass of people. The noise from their chatter flew upward. Several bookies waved slips of paper in the air and a gaggle of gamblers crowded around them.

Kane glanced at the crowd, then at Imogen. She wondered if he was suppressing a shudder.

"Cheers," he said, tipping his flute to hers. "Here's to Ascot."

"And for being away from the crowd." Imogen smiled and took a sip of the wonderfully light, fizzy liquid. "Have you been here before?" she asked.

"I have been to races before, Brunei being the last one if I remember correctly. But never Ascot."

"It's wonderful."

"I hoped you would enjoy it."

"I am. I will." Imogen watched as several horses cantered past on the outer edge of the course toward the starting line. The jockeys stood high in their stirrups and wore bright satin outfits with numbers on their backs. "The thing is, though, Kane." She pulled in a deep breath. "I'm at your disposal; you don't need to treat me to fancy days out to have my business advice."

"Mmm... I have you at my disposal," he said, nodding slowly and not taking his attention off her. "Now there's a temptation."

She frowned a little, though not in annoyance, more in confusion. He had a mischievous glint in his eyes she hadn't seen before. "You know what I meant."

"I'll pretend that I do." He sipped on his drink, a smile hovering on his lips. "But today you're my guest."

"Which is very flattering, but you said you wanted to discuss your new venture."

"And indeed I do. But after we've eaten. There's plenty of time for work talk." He glanced at the girl who held the champagne tray and gave her a quick nod.

"Are you sure?" Imogen asked. "I'm happy to eat and talk shop."

"Well, I'm not. I'd much rather talk about you."

"Really?" She couldn't help the surprise in her voice.

"Yes. Tell me, where did you grow up? Do you have any brothers or sisters? What led you into the world of banking?"

"I thought you'd have found all of that stuff out when you did my background check."

"Well, let's just say I didn't."

She frowned.

*Had he?*

"I didn't," he said with a slight shrug. "Tell me about you, Imogen Patricia White, not the bank manager who is at my beck and call, apparently, but you, what's in there." He nodded at her chest, his gaze lingering on the inch of cleavage on show. "What's inside?"

For a moment Imogen felt a flush on her neck, but she turned to the light breeze and took a sip of drink, squashing the feeling away. "Not much to tell. I grew up in Southend, always wanted to move to the city, and when I was eighteen I did. I completed a BSc in economics with a placement at Coutts, and they took me on as soon as I graduated. That was eleven years ago, and now I'm the youngest female to ever run a city branch."

"That's very impressive."

"Kind of you to say so, but what you've achieved is also pretty impressive."

He smiled. "I'm glad you think that."

"I do."

There was a brief pause, then, "You omitted to tell me about siblings."

"I'm an only child." She paused. "You?"

"I have one brother, Taylor. I'm a little older than him and I knew he'd be snapping at my ankles as soon as he could. I suppose he stoked my competitive streak. We're as determined as each other when it comes to success and building empires."

"And what an empire. You have a remarkable list of assets."

"I don't like to feel as though I'm missing out on anything." He shrugged, as though competitiveness was a trait he was a slave to, yet enjoyed. "If something's hot I want a slice of the action."

"Perhaps you should go into horse racing. Build your own track with a path directly from the heliport that's just for you."

"Don't tempt me." He gave a small laugh then turned. "Our lunch is here."

Imogen's stomach threatened to growl as the smell of sweet onions and freshly baked bread wafted toward her.

Kane directed her back inside, out of the glare of the sun, and she allowed a smartly dressed waiter to pull out her chair and seat her.

She looked at the large white dish that held delicate slivers of smoked salmon on a bed of salad leaves. Around the edge was a drizzle of lemon-colored sauce and a warm bread roll on a side plate.

"This looks lovely," Imogen said. "Salmon is my favorite."

"I aim to please." Kane slipped off his jacket and handed it to the waiter. He sat, shook out his large napkin, then placed it on his knee.

Imogen leaned back and allowed another waiter to gracefully drop hers into place. Had Kane known salmon was her favorite fish? She couldn't resist it on any menu.

She wouldn't put it past him to have found that out about her if he really had been making enquiries. It wasn't exactly a secret in the office that she was predictable with her meal choices on staff nights out. But would he have? Was he really that thorough in checking out his inner circle? No, it was a coincidence, that's all—wasn't it?

She pushed the thought from her mind and began to eat, enjoying the fresh, fragrant flavors and the exquisite fish that melted on her tongue.

"But you still didn't tell me what's in your heart," Kane said, slicing a bread roll in half.

"What do you mean?"

"What are your dreams for the future?"

"That's a big question."

"So give me a big answer."

"Professionally, I've achieved a lot more than I thought I would, but I would like to continue up the career ladder. There's more opportunity for promotion, including joining the board. It's a hard position to get, but I'd like to be the first woman there."

"That sounds like an excellent goal." He stabbed a piece of salmon. "And what about men? No banker boyfriend on the scene?"

Imogen held his gaze. "No. No banker boyfriend." She paused. "No any boyfriend."

"You astound me." He didn't look surprised.

Had he known she was single?—yes, of course he had.

"How come a beautiful woman like you hasn't been whisked off her feet?"

She refused to break his steady eye contact. "Because I haven't allowed anyone to take my feet from under me. I can stand up on my own perfectly well."

For a moment she thought he'd snap back a clever answer. But he didn't. He tipped his head and laughed. A great big guffaw that came up from his belly and rumbled around the large room. "Well, you are just priceless, and I should have expected that," he said, wiping the corner of his mouth on his napkin.

"Why?" she said, not sure what had been the reason for such mirth. It was true, she hadn't found time to date because no one had convinced her they were worth the slot in her schedule. An occasional one-night stand could sort out an itch, just to stop her from feeling completely celibate, but overall she was happy to be single. "Why should you have expected that?"

"Because you're not the type of person to do anything you don't want to, including falling in love," he said.

She had fallen in love once, a long time ago, but he didn't need to know that. "So how come there is no Mrs. Kane Ward?" she asked.

"Fair enough." He nodded, then put a forkful of food into his mouth. When he'd finished eating he said, "I thought there would be once upon a time, but it seemed I couldn't give her what she needed."

"But you could give her anything?" Imogen tried not to feel jealous of this faceless woman who'd nearly netted Kane Ward.

"Ah, that's where you're wrong. I could have given her anything money could buy. But that wasn't what she wanted. She wanted my time, more than I was able to give her."

"Time." She paused. "So your work, your empire and the running of it got in the way of the relationship."

"It more than got in the way of it. It was the reason it ended." He glanced out at the racetrack and picked up his drink. "But that's ancient history. She is with another do— man now."

"It's easy to fall into the belief, in our lines of work, that being rich equates happiness."

"Sensible words, Imogen. Wealth bring status and it can make being unhappy a whole lot less miserable, but it won't make you happy."

Imogen set down her knife and fork on her empty plate. "Are you unhappy, Kane?" Damn, she hoped she wasn't speaking out of turn. But they were sharing, talking about love and the past.

"No," he said, turning back to her. "I'm not unhappy at all." He paused.

"So does that mean you're happy?"

"Right now, this minute." He smiled suddenly. "Yes. How could I not be? I'm at the races, I have wonderful company and fantastic Michelin star food."

"And if you had to lose one of those things?"

He thought for a moment. "The races. We could be anywhere enjoying each other, good food and having a wonderful date."

"Date?" Her mouth stayed open a fraction.

"Ahhh…" He sat back and folded his arms. "I've been rumbled."

"Is this a date?" She'd been emphatic to Clarris that it was business.

"Would you like it to be?"

"I'm on work time. I…" She wasn't on a date with Kane Ward. That was ridiculous. She was here in a professional capacity. Wasn't she?

"Is that a yes or a no?" He raised his eyebrows and an amused flash crossed his eyes.

"But you said... the business venture. You wanted to discuss it."

"Back to that. Okay. Shall we get the business matter out of the way?"

Imogen paused as a waiter topped up their drinks, cleared their plates, then left them alone.

"Maybe it would be for the best?" She could feel her head swimming slightly and it wasn't just the champagne. It was also the realization that Clarris had been right. Kane Ward had tricked her into going on a date with him. A date at Royal Ascot, no less, and in a private catered viewing box—no doubt the most expensive and exclusive available. She should have seen the signs, recognized the hints. Instead, she'd fixated on the word business and had gone along with it all.

If her superiors at Coutts could see her now?

"So this new venture," she said. "What's the deal?"

"Clubs."

"As in night clubs?"

"They'll be open at night, yes." He nodded slowly.

"And where are you planning on opening?"

"So far I have earmarked locations in London, Berlin, and Rome." As he said each one, he tapped his finger on the table.

"Good choices."

"This type of... hospitality venture is new to me. It's more personal, it feels like I want to put an accent of myself into it."

"As in manage it? On the ground?"

"Good heavens, no. I'll have full staff at each club. I mean I want to have more than usual input into the creation of them. The layout, the equipment, the décor."

Imogen nodded. "I can understand that." Though she couldn't believe he had much input into the interior design of his chain of hotels. She could almost imagine him waving his hand at a subordinate and saying 'do your stuff.'

"And that's where you come in." He leaned forward and steepled his fingers under his chin.

"How can I help?"

"I need you to come to an existing club with me. I suppose you could say a rival club, except that I know the owner very well and consider him a good friend."

"How would that be of use to you?"

"Because…" He paused. "I need a female perspective. A feminine angle when it comes to designing my own playground."

*Playground?*

Imogen couldn't help but wonder if this was all a ruse to get her to agree to another date with him.

"You see," he went on, "I want my clubs to appeal to both men and women, and I fear I may be too heavy-handed on the masculinity. I don't want to make it hard and unwelcoming for the softer sex."

"What about an interior designer?"

"Oh, no, that wouldn't do at all." He held his hands up. "It has to be you."

"But, surely someone trained—"

"No. I want you to do it." He'd spoken in a very authoritative tone, as if the decision was already set in stone.

The waiter appeared with two fresh plates of food.

As he set them down, Imogen took a moment to digest what Kane was saying. He really was being very adamant about her help, and only *her* help. Which she was happy to give, if it was all on the straight and narrow and wouldn't mean she was skiving off work, which today was feeling decidedly like she was.

"It's rather an unusual service for Coutts to offer," she said when they were alone again. "But it's not unreasonable as long as you know I'm no expert in décor." She thought of her messy apartment that was all about function and comfort rather than style.

"You might surprise yourself." He held up his glass. "To teamwork."

She clinked. "Teamwork."

"Oh, and by the way. This club you're going to be visiting, Imogen. It's in New York City."

"New York?" she said, almost spluttering on her champagne.

"Yes. I'm afraid even I can't arrange to have the entire club brought to London."

"But—?"

"You might have to take some time off work. Unless, of course, you can persuade your department that it's all business."

"And is it?"

"I'm hoping there will be some pleasure to be had." He picked up his knife and fork and cut into a steak that appeared as soft as butter. He kept his concentration down, as if trying to make his comment non-suggestive.

But it was as suggestive as hell. Fuck, just Kane saying the word pleasure sent a bolt of heat over her neck and cheeks that threatened to come to boiling point.

He glanced up at her. A sensual smile tugged at his mouth even though he was chewing. He knew damn well the effect his words had had on her.

"Okay," she said, tipping her chin and refusing to be embarrassed by her flush. Though she did hope her nipples weren't pressing against the inside of her dress and poking out. "I'll come with you. When do we fly?"

# CHAPTER FOUR

Imogen stared out of the limo window at the majestic skyscrapers. This was her first time in Manhattan, though she'd been to the United States on business before. "This is like a movie set," she said, imagining King Kong swinging from the top of the Empire State Building.

"I often think that too," Kane said.

Feeling the heat of his attention, she turned to him.

As she'd suspected, he was staring straight at her, the angle of his jaw set tight and his chin tilted. He wore a black short-sleeved shirt and dark jeans, teamed with a lightweight leather jacket. She'd thought many times on their journey over the Atlantic how gorgeous he'd looked. She'd also caught one of the flight attendants on his private jet giving him an appreciative glance and even suspected a female passenger at the airport had taken a sneaky photograph.

She crossed her legs as a bubble of excitement spun in her belly and her short pencil skirt hitched up her thigh. *She* was the woman sitting with Kane Ward. *She* had his attention. She wasn't sure exactly why or for how long or what he really wanted from her, but she was happy to go with it while it lasted. What the hell did she have to lose?

Since their day at Ascot, she'd been thinking more and

more about the undercurrents of his quietly spoken words. The words about pleasure that seemed to hum right through her every time she remembered them. And what exactly was this club that only she could help with?

Naturally, thoughts of Kane had drifted into fantasies of him getting hot and sweaty and using those damn fine hands of his on her. She'd woken in the middle of the night on two occasions with erotic dreams—him as the star—still vivid in her mind. She'd reached beneath the sheets, spread her legs, and brought herself to swift, frantic orgasms while calling out his name and imagining him pounding into her.

She looked at him now, studied the way the flick of his hair licked over his brow and how his neatly cut, slim sideburns fed down into his facial hair. What would he think if she told him about her nighttime activities? Would he dismiss her as a fool for believing she had a chance—that he would ever touch her like that? Or would it turn him on? Would he get hard, create a fantasy of his own about her, reach into his trousers and touch himself the way she had?

She knew which option she'd prefer. How she'd like him to think of her as a sexual woman and not just a banker.

"I will take you," he said quietly, leaning a little closer.

Her heart rate picked up and the hairs around the base of her neck tingled. She could feel his body heat spreading over her arm through the cool air conditioning of the car. "Take me?"

"Yes." His gaze slipped down her chest to the tops of her legs.

She followed his line of sight and saw that the very tip of her sheer stocking was displayed from the hem of her skirt. It was delicate and made of ghost-thin white lace.

"I will take you..." he repeated and placed the tip of his index finger on her knee. "There."

Imogen caught her breath. It was as if all of her nerves zoned in on her right kneecap. Her skin positively buzzed, even with this tiny physical connection to Kane.

"There?" she managed as he drifted his finger oh, so

gently up her right thigh and let it settle over the lace of her stocking. God, if just his finger could make her feel like ripping her clothes off, what would…?

"Yes," he said, leaning closer still, "there, up the Empire State Building. I'll take you as high as you want to go." His breath had warmed her cheek as he'd whispered the last words, drawing them out long and slow.

*As high as she wanted to go?*

"Okay." She studied the black stubble growing over his top lip and the way his lashes spread finely around his almond-shaped eyes. He was tired, like she was, but still, a heat, no, a raging fire burned in their depths. "I'd like that," she managed. "To go to the top."

"Oh, I can do top very well," he said, looking back up at her face. "Very well indeed."

He moved his finger higher still, her skirt bunching around it in a series of wrinkles. His gaze seemed to penetrate right through her. As if he were trying to see into her psyche and determine what effect he had on her.

The effect was she knew without doubt they'd moved from the realms of professionalism into a whole other area. An area where nothing was certain and excitement and lust reigned.

*What had she gotten into?*

Her whole leg tingled and she tightened her internal muscles. She was getting turned on, just from this. He was making it very obvious what he wanted.

The same thing she did.

The right side of his mouth twitched into a smile and his eyes narrowed.

Imogen fought to stop herself panting. Yes, she wanted him. Her bones ached from her wanting him. But even so, she didn't want to look desperate. She needed to retain a modicum of dignity.

"Kane," she managed.

"I'm sorry," he said, his mouth hovering over hers. "But all that way on the plane, all I wanted to do was find out if…"

"Find out what?" She stared into his eyes.

"Find out if you were wearing stockings." His eyelids drooped, as though the knowledge had drugged him.

"I am."

"I know that now." Instead of just his finger, he placed his palm over the lacy trim. "And I'm so glad you are."

The heat of his flesh burned through her. She clamped her legs tighter together. Her pussy was dampening and her breasts felt heavy. It was getting harder to breathe.

"It means all those times I met with you," he said, "and wondered if you had sexy undergarments on beneath the prim suits, I was right."

"You… you thought of that?"

He swallowed "Is that so hard to believe?"

"Well, I…" She paused. "Kane… why have you brought me here?"

"I told you. I need your help." He rubbed around the top of her thigh until his fingers caught on the seat.

"And… anything else?"

"That remains to be seen." He lifted his hand and smoothed her skirt back into place. It was an industrial move, performing a task. The caress had gone.

Imogen's heart raced. Her mind was full of blustering, excited thoughts. It hadn't taken long from touchdown at JFK to him letting her know that he was definitely interested in more than her business acumen.

"On what?" she asked. "Depends on what?"

"Ah, here we are." He straightened and looked out of the window. He shifted away and unclipped his belt.

The car was drawn to a halt and the engine died.

"It's not my regular New York place; my brother is staying there while he oversees a new venture," he said. "But I think we'll be very comfortable in the penthouse of The Four Seasons."

"What?" Imogen was aghast. "Yes. I would think so." She'd never in a million years thought she'd stay in The Four

Seasons' penthouse. It was legendary and more than a budget blower, it would bankrupt her.

A valet opened the car door and Kane stepped out. He turned and offered his hand.

Imogen took it and allowed him to support her as she stood. Instantly, the noise of car engines and a melody of horns flooded her ears. Warmth filled her nostrils—air infused with exhaust fumes, sweet scents of food, and a medley of things she didn't recognize.

She glanced up at the hotel. An ornate metal canopy protected arriving guests from the elements, and huge flags were hanging from above enormous dark windows. She'd stayed in nice hotels before, but knew this was really going to be something special.

"Imogen," Kane said. "Are you ready?"

She took her hand from his and adjusted the strap of her purse over her shoulder. "Yes, yes, of course."

He smiled.

As the driver and valet unloaded the luggage, Imogen followed Kane through revolving doors into the lobby.

"Wow," she said, staring at the magnificent staircase in front of her and the colossal pillars either side. The floor was a work of art in itself, and the scent of vanilla and sandalwood took the place of the outdoor city smells.

Kane turned to her, his smile still in place.

"I'm sorry," she said, feeling a little foolish. "But you've probably stayed in a million beautiful hotels, and I've enjoyed a few, but this is something else."

"It is the best," he said, "which is why we're here."

"Good afternoon, Mr. Ward." A concierge walked toward them.

"Good afternoon," Kane said.

"If you'd like to come this way, I'll show you to the Ty Warner suite. Your luggage will be right behind us."

"Thank you," Kane said.

Imogen looked at him. He appeared to drift through life and from one place to another effortlessly. Not having to lower himself with mundane tasks like checking in, or even giving his name. When they'd arrived at the airport, their progress through private security had been incredibly efficient and when they'd disembarked and walked through JFK, their luggage was already in the waiting limousine.

"This is the suite's private elevator." The concierge pressed a button and the doors slid silently open. "It has a pin number, which you can find by the telephone in the suite. You'll need to use it each time."

"Thank you," Kane said, slipping his hand onto Imogen's back. "Please, you first." He urged her forward.

She stepped in. What would the suite be like? And more to the point, what were the sleeping arrangements? Did it have two bedrooms? Was Kane planning on sharing a bed with her?

Would she complain?

*Hell, no.*

The concierge hit the top level and Imogen's stomach dropped a little as they were whizzed upward. No one spoke. The concierge stared at the door, apparently waiting for it to open. Kane removed his hand from her back.

She caught his gaze in the smoky mirrors. He was staring at her reflection.

She glanced away, not wanting him to read her mind about the bedroom situation. She didn't want to be too damn transparent.

The suite, on the fifty-second floor, was breathtaking. Imogen walked in, held in another gasp of appreciation but couldn't help staring. It had extravagance that she'd never experienced before. Artwork, antiques, a grand piano set in an alcove with floor-to-ceiling windows and views of Manhattan. It wasn't sparse and minimalist as she'd thought it might be; it was full of luxury, from immaculate furniture, beautiful paintings, and intricate sculptures.

It also had several rooms. She could see a bedroom to the right and another to the left.

Kane tipped the concierge, who immediately retreated to

the elevator.

Kane walked to the left, slipped off his jacket, and draped it casually over a shiny brown leather sofa.

"You will be in here," he said, pushing open the door to the bedroom on her left. "I trust you will be comfortable."

So they weren't sharing a room. That cleared that up then.

Was she disappointed or relieved? After what had just happened in the car, how she'd felt when he'd touched her knee... disappointment was the overwhelming emotion.

Perhaps he was being polite. Maybe things would heat up.

A girl could hope.

Imogen looked inside her bedroom. It was huge and also had enormous windows with priceless views of the city. The bed was vast and had cream and gold covers. A sleek dressing table was set against the wall, several straight-backed chairs were dotted about, and in a silver ice bucket there was a bottle of champagne.

"I'm sure I will be," she said, admiring the picture hanging behind the bed. "It's beautiful."

"You should rest," he said. "Before we go to the club tonight."

"Yes. That would be sensible." She was weary, her eyes heavy; however, the excitement of the last few minutes, in the cab and arriving at the suite, had perked her up. She could probably keep going. "But—?"

"I insist. Besides, I have someone I must spend time with now."

"You do?" She was surprised and wanted to demand to know who. But it wasn't really any of her business.

"Yes." He studied her and tipped his head slightly. "My sensei."

"Sensei?"

"Karate master. I would never come to New York without studying with him. Apart from the fact it is to my advantage, it would also be very discourteous of me."

"You do karate?" Imogen was surprised. She'd never thought of Kane as having a hobby like martial arts. He was always so busy. But then again, if she was going to pick one sport for him to practice, then yes, it would be karate, something that required absolute self-control and discipline, not to mention skillful hands and precision timing.

"It wouldn't do my body any good to sit behind a desk all day," he said, "and besides, I like knowing that I can look after myself and others, should the need arise."

"Yes, I agree." She paused. "Are you a black belt?" The image of him in a starched white outfit wearing a tight black belt and with a sheen of sweat on his brow sprang into her mind. She'd never thought of karate as sexy before, but right now, she couldn't think of anything more erotic. His dark hair set against all that white, his feet bare and his muscles tense...

He nodded. "Several times over."

"Oh." She didn't know what that meant. "Well, that's good."

He smiled. "Please, help yourself to champagne, or if you'd rather something else, just call down for room service. Whatever you want. When I return we'll head to the club." He glanced at his watch. "Three hours. Yes, that will be about right. Please be ready to go."

It hadn't sounded like a request, more of a command. "Okay."

The sound of the elevator doors pinging reminded Imogen of their luggage. She'd have to see if the little black dress she'd brought would need ironing.

"Your outfit for tonight should be in here." Kane strode across the large bedroom and pulled open the door of a tall cupboard.

Imogen couldn't see inside from where she was standing.

"Ah, yes, good, perfect in fact," he said, shutting the door again with a click.

"I have an outfit, in there?" she asked, raising her

eyebrows. "But I brought one to wear."

"I'm sure you did. But I think this one will be very flattering and also it means you will blend in."

"Blend in?"

"Yes."

He walked back over to her, came up close, so close she could have reached up and stroked her finger down his cheek.

"I don't want us to stand out," he said. "We need to be discreet so you can experience without distraction. Tonight it's just looking, no touching."

*No touching?*

"Oh, I see." She didn't really, only now she was itching to look at the outfit he'd bought her, but his eyes were like magnets, and when he set his whole attention on her, like he had now, she found it impossible to tear herself away.

"Just looking, no touching," he repeated.

Imogen swallowed. Her right leg tingled—the spot where he'd caressed her in the car.

He suddenly stepped away and turned.

She stared at his broad shoulders and the way his black shirt tapered to the waistband of his jeans.

"Be ready," he said, pulling the door closed behind him.

Silence enveloped her.

Imogen pursed her lips and blew out a long breath. Whenever Kane left a room it was as though an electric current had been switched off. His energy was extreme. He both fascinated and confused her. He turned her on to the point she felt combustion was a definite possibility and also made her want to put up a shield to protect herself from his power—the power he had over her. A control that seemed to be growing by the minute.

He'd bought her an outfit? What the hell was that all about?

She frowned at the cupboard. First he'd told her what to wear to the races. Admittedly, it had been perfect for the occasion. And now he'd given her something to wear to the club. She'd never let a man have any say in how she dressed before. That wasn't the type of woman she was. Imogen made her own decisions, her own choices.

She kicked off her heels and sank her aching feet into the soft carpet. She went to the cupboard and pulled open the door.

Hanging in the shadows was a short black leather dress.

Imogen bit on her bottom lip. Okay. So she'd gone for a little black dress too, but this...

She held the dress up to the window. The leather material was shiny, it had the thinnest shoulder straps and it was so short she knew it would barely cover her knickers once it was on. But what really caught her attention was the intricate corset detail that ran down the front. Tiny laces that appeared to hold the dress together, and each one threaded through bright red eyelets.

Her mouth dried.

She couldn't wear this.

It was... tarty.

Yes, that was the word for it. Or was it? Because actually it was beyond tarty, it was kind of fetishy. Kinky.

*Bloody hell.*

She rubbed her fingers over her brow and continued to stare at it.

Kane Ward wanted her to wear this provocative, ultra-sexy dress tonight when they went out. And what's more, he'd said it would mean she'd blend in. Yes, that had been his words. *Blend in.*

So everyone else would be wearing things like this?

This was no ordinary club.

But why did that surprise her? Kane was no ordinary man, and this was no ordinary business trip.

She knew that much already.

She walked to the huge window and held the dress up. The light caught on the super-smooth surface as she moved it left to right then slid her hand down the front. Despite being leather, it was wonderfully soft, the material almost paper-thin. It wouldn't feel stiff on her body, she was sure. It would be more like a second skin.

She juddered out a breath.

Maybe she should just decline the trip to the club. Or perhaps insist on wearing the dress she'd brought. That was plain and neat, and although short in length, it at least made an attempt to reach her knees.

She walked around in a circle, worrying at her bottom lip and swinging the hanger from her finger.

What would Kane say if he came back and she wasn't in this dress?

Tough. She couldn't be told what to wear. She *wouldn't* be told what to wear.

But something inside her didn't want to disappoint him. He wanted to see her in this dress, the way he'd wanted to see her in something pretty when he'd taken her to the races. Plus, she'd loved his sexy satisfied smile when he'd seen her at the helipad.

Her heart was longing to see that smile again. She wanted to please him. Here. In New York. Where it felt like anything could happen. Even wearing this crazy little dress.

It wasn't as if she didn't have the figure for it and it certainly looked to be her size.

"I should wear it." She nodded and placed it over the end of a chaise longue. "Yes. I'll try it on, and if it's okay, I'll wear it."

Feeling like she'd made some kind of decision and a celebration was called for, Imogen pulled the champagne from the ice bucket. She dug her nail into the foil around the bottle of Krug and popped the cork. It flew a few feet into the air, then rolled beneath the dressing table.

A slightly hysterical laugh bubbled up from her chest, but it caught in her throat as froth slipped over the rim. "Whoops."

She reached for a flute and poured.

Who would have thought this time last week when she was number crunching and wading through tax returns that now she would be in the penthouse at The Four Seasons in New York, planning some kind of kinky night out with Kane Ward. Yes, she needed a drink.

She took a sip of the chilled, sparkling liquid.

"Mmm…" She wandered to a large door that was slightly ajar and pushed it open. Inside was the most lavish, decadent bathroom she'd ever seen. It appeared to have been created out of gold-hued marble, had a huge shower cubicle, several sinks beneath a giant mirror, and a bath that she could almost swim lengths in.

Like all the other rooms in the suite, it had floor-to-ceiling windows so it was possible to lounge in the bath and admire the Empire State Building.

Imogen didn't hesitate to start the bath filling. She tipped a whole bottle of sweetly scented foaming liquid into the stream of water, then began to strip off her clothes.

Within minutes she was sinking into the hot water. It surrounded her tired body like a blanket, wrapping around her sore feet, her stiff legs, and up to her breasts.

She swooshed the bubbles around, splashing them over her nipples, then sighed and reached for her drink.

Staring out at the view, she rested her head back.

She'd read a book about kink a while ago. A couple who engaged in bondage and spanking. The hero would get rough with the heroine, but she'd loved it, lapped it up. Taken whatever he'd given her.

Was that the kind of man Kane was? Like the hero in that kinky book? Damn, what was its name, that book?

She frowned. The title wasn't important. What was important was to find out if the man she was getting hot for was into bondage and spanking?

And if so… was she?

# CHAPTER FIVE

Imogen knew she wouldn't sleep if she rested on the bed so was content to laze in the bath for an hour or so. She let the water soak away her tiredness as her mind spun with thoughts of Kane and what the night would bring.

Eventually, she rose from the water, ready to put on *that* dress.

A bottle of rich, sweet body lotion tempted Imogen, and she slathered herself with it before hunting out satin knickers from her suitcase. She found the little black number she'd planned on wearing and decided to hang it up—it would be okay to wear another night and hanging might drop the creases.

Something at the base of the cupboard caught her attention.

Boots.

Very long, thigh-length boots.

She picked them up by the tops. They were made of the same wonderfully soft leather as the dress and had identical corset-style ties up the front, including the tiny red eyelets.

"Bloody hell!"

The dress she'd been prepared to give a go, but these... well, these were just too much.

She flicked them over and examined the three-inch heels.

Heels weren't an issue, but even she'd have to concentrate to walk on those tiny points.

She glanced at the dress. Together the two items screamed *slut, come fuck me, I'm a sure thing*. She may as well just have trollop stamped on her forehead.

They were all the things she most definitely wasn't.

But did Kane *want* her to be?

No, surely not. If he'd wanted a slut he could have found one easily enough. But he'd chosen her and he knew damn well she was a professional with a reputation to protect for the sake of her career.

What if someone from London saw her out, in this get-up?

Had he even thought of that? She knew many people in the industry, many based in the US. It was a slim possibility, but still... it was a possibility.

She placed the boots by the dress and backed away from them. She picked up her brush and began to pull it through her damp hair as she stared at the outfit.

Kane didn't date sluts. She knew that. It was clearly more complicated than that he wanted a tartily dressed woman on his arm.

Or was it? Maybe that was what he was into. His kink could very well be slutty outfits—whore fantasy might be what got him off.

Imogen poured herself another glass of champagne, knocked half of it back in one go then sat, in just her knickers, at the dressing table. She set about pinning her hair high and trying to figure out what was going on.

Kane was a complex man, there was no doubt about that. He also liked to keep things close to his chest. He only revealed what he needed to and what he wanted to.

But could she get him to reveal more?

The rise of a challenge swelled in her chest. Imogen hadn't got where she was by being afraid of finding out what was going on. She also liked order, knowing what was what.

So yes, she'd wear the dress.

And the boots.

*The boots?*

She glanced at them again.

*Damn it.*

She wanted to.

She didn't want to.

She took another glug of champagne.

She'd see how she felt once she had the dress on. That was the best plan at this stage.

She reached for a bright red lipstick, twisted it up to a point, and began to carefully apply it.

• • • • • • •

As the sun set and the New York City downtown lights twinkled through the window, Imogen stared at herself in the mirror.

The dress did indeed fit perfectly. It made her breasts appear voluptuous, and because of the way it nipped in at her waist, it gave her hips a seriously sexy flare.

God, this was the look he wanted on her? That thought was both thrilling and frightening.

The boots complemented the dress beautifully. They were made to go together. They rose well beyond her knees, showing only a few inches of bare thigh before the lofty hem of the dress, which, as predicted, only just covered her underwear.

She skimmed her hand over her stomach and turned to survey her behind.

Damn it. Her mother would never have let her out in this. And her father, well, he'd turn in his grave.

What was she doing?

But it did look good. She could pull it off. She could work this look if it was what Kane wanted and would allow her to get to the bottom of his kink—if indeed that's what this business arrangement was all about.

*Kink.*

She smiled. She actually really liked the outfit. Did that mean she was kinky too? Perhaps it did. But so what if she was. Maybe it was time to let that side of her out to play.

She reached for her drink, realized she'd downed yet another glass of champagne, and hiccupped. She should have some water; then maybe she wouldn't be so brazen about unearthing whatever kinks and knots lay in her psyche.

After drinking a big glass of water, Imogen added a necklace then earrings to her outfit for good measure. They were a sapphire set that she'd planned on wearing with the other dress. Not quite in style with the leather number she'd opted for, but maybe it gave her a classy-slut appearance—if there was such a thing.

The water rehydrated her and the champagne glow eased. It was dark outside, so she decided to go and wait for Kane in the lounge area and enjoy the view from there.

She hadn't heard him come back from karate, but the door to the other bedroom was now shut and the lamps at either end of the sofas were on, giving a gentle glow to the elegant room.

She stood still for a moment, wondering if she'd hear him moving about, but she didn't. There was no noise coming from anywhere in the apartment; it was totally silent.

The piano stood grandly in its glass alcove. Imogen pulled out the burgundy-colored velvet stool and twisted it to face the city. She sat and took in the panoramic view. The Chrysler Building loomed large, the Empire State larger, and all around were interesting rooftops to study. It was a sight she'd never thought she'd get to sit and admire from somewhere so sumptuous and exclusive.

"Imogen."

She started slightly at the sound of Kane's deep voice right behind her.

"I didn't hear you come back," she said, forcing herself

not to turn. She continued to stare outside, chin tipped.

"I did." He rested his hand on her left shoulder. "Come back, that is."

The heat from his palm seeped onto her skin and seemed to slide up her neck. The hairs at her nape tingled.

His wrist was in her peripheral vision. He appeared to be wearing a black jacket and the cuff of a white shirt peeked from beneath it.

He slipped his hand down her chest, not indecently low, his fingers just past her collarbone. It sent tingles of arousal around her body and her breasts shifted upward as she breathed deep.

"You look beautiful," he said quietly.

She continued to stare at the window. She could make out his reflection. He was looking down at her, head bent, and she'd been right, he was wearing a suit—a tuxedo complete with a bow tie.

He was the most handsome man she'd ever seen.

"Thank you," she managed. "This style of dress isn't something I'd usually wear."

"I know, which is why I had it made for you."

"Made for me?"

"Yes. Made. Exactly to order. And the boots too."

Imogen crossed and uncrossed her legs. The dress shifted, showing an extra inch of thigh. There was nothing she could do about it short of tugging, which she knew would be to no avail.

He pulled in a breath, blew it out. The breeze of air tickled over her head.

"The boots are..." she said.

"Wonderfully kinky," he finished for her.

"Yes. Kinky."

There, it was out in the open.

"And look exquisite on you." He slipped his hand a little lower, until his fingertips rested on the first inch of material of her dress.

The moment was electric yet delicate. As though they

were encased in glass that might shatter if either moved too fast or spoke too loud.

"We're going to a kinky club, aren't we?" she asked in barely a whisper. "That's the kind of club you're setting up, isn't it?"

"Is that a problem?"

Was that a problem? No, she guessed it wasn't. She was curious, that's why it wasn't a problem. And it certainly put a new spin on their trip. "No, I don't think so."

"You don't think so?"

"I just..."

"You're just worried about being seen in this stunning outfit."

"Well, it's not likely I'd see anyone I know, but still, I'd rather my seniors..."

"You worry too much. I have it all organized." He slipped his other hand around her neck, swept up the column of her throat and cupped her chin. "I'll take care of you. When you're with me, I'll always take care of you. You don't need to concern yourself with anything."

Imogen closed her eyes. A soft sigh escaped her lips. She believed him, she really did. Kane was the most competent man she'd ever met. If he said he'd look after her, then he would.

And his hands, hands that he could use as weapons, hands that ruled a business empire, hands that now skimmed her flesh, held her face. She didn't want him to ever stop touching her.

"You have to believe that," he went on in a low murmur. "That while you're mine you will only ever feel good, only ever be treated with the utmost respect and consideration."

"Yes," she managed.

*His?*

He slid his hand lower over her dress to the rise of her breast. "Imogen." He tilted her head farther up, his fingers pressing gently on her throat. "Do you trust me?"

"I think so."

For a moment he was quiet, then, "That's a good start." He stroked his thumb across her cheek and placed his lips by her ear. "But before we do anything else I need you to wear one more thing."

Imogen breathed in his cologne, spicy and sexy. Her breasts ached with desire, her abdomen clenched, and her clitoris tingled with need. What else could she possibly wear?

He lifted his touch from her face and chest and carefully released the clasp on her necklace.

She opened her eyes and again studied his reflection as he set it aside, atop the piano.

"In order for us to truly blend in tonight," he said, "I need you to wear a different adornment on your neck." He stood directly behind her and plucked something from his pocket.

Imogen couldn't see what.

But she didn't wonder for long. He circled her head with his arms and held a thin strip of leather in front of her with a small red metal buckle and several holes. It appeared to be a collar.

"What is it?" she asked, her attention fixated on it.

"It's a symbol that you belong to me," he said. "So at the club you won't get pestered by other doms."

She opened her mouth to speak. Questions were piling up on her tongue. A collar? Belong to him? Other doms?

"I'm sorry," he said. "I'm sure you have a million things you want to ask me, and yes, I'm probably moving too fast. But this is all quite necessary and we have all night for you to ask me whatever you want to."

Imogen closed her mouth.

"So may I?" he asked. "Put my collar on you?"

She nodded.

Kane slipped it around her neck. The leather was cool on her skin, which had heated where his hand had rested.

He fastened it, not tight, but not loose either. She swallowed and moved her head slightly, testing the feel of restriction at her throat. It was strange, constraining but also oddly comforting.

"How is it?" he asked.

"Okay."

He moved in front of her, his hands at his sides and his feet slightly apart.

She looked up at him.

He tipped his head, as though waiting for her to say more.

"I will know it's there all night," she said. "It's comfortable but... there."

He smiled, as though she'd said the right thing. "Good. That is how it should feel."

Imogen got that familiar pleasant glow in her chest. She'd pleased him. Said the right thing. He always rewarded her with a softness in his voice and a genuine smile. It made her want to please him more, in any way she could.

"Stand," he said. "Let me see you."

She did as he'd asked and realized as she straightened that she was almost as tall as him in her heels.

He bit on the inside of his cheek and nodded. His gaze slipped down her body, right to her toes then back up again.

Imogen resisted the urge to fiddle with her collar and instead placed her hand on her waist and jutted her hip out.

He chuckled. "Yes, that's it. I knew you were a natural."

"A natural slut?"

The humor left his features. A frown plowed over his brow. "Oh, no, not a slut, never a slut."

"What then? Why a dress and boots that would be perfectly suited to Soho?"

He stepped close and took her hand. With his other he opened her fingers so her palm was flat and facing upward. He raised it to his lips and kissed the center. "Imogen, this outfit shows you off as a woman. It doesn't mean, not in my world, that you're available; in fact, the collar, as I've just explained, means the opposite." He closed her fingers and wrapped his big hand over hers. "This dress, those boots, they allow you to let your sexuality breathe. Tonight prim suits don't exist. Tonight there is only space for celebrating female allure and pleasure, which, of course, is the point of all of this."

"The point?"

He smiled. "I need your help, remember. You're right, I wish to set up similar clubs, but need a female perspective. *Your* perspective." He released her and stepped away, glanced at his watch. "Come. We have work to do."

Imogen turned, watched him retrieve a small black bag from the table, then go to the elevator.

That had put her in her place.

They had work to do.

It was time to go.

*His world. Allowing her sexuality to breathe. Female allure.*

She steeled herself. That's why she was here, for work—to help Kane Ward with his next business venture.

She tugged at the collar and spotted her necklace abandoned on the piano.

She was in New York City dressed in kinky gear, and on top of all that, she now looked like his pet.

Damn it. She should probably ask for a raise.

# CHAPTER SIX

Kane stopped at a black door with a golden-colored number sixty-nine placed in the center.

He pressed the buzzer.

A small red light came on, indicating someone had responded to his arrival.

"Black River caviar," Kane said into the speaker.

A click signaled the lock being released.

"Is that a password?" Imogen asked.

"Yes, it changes every night."

"How do you know what it is tonight?"

"It was given to me when I put our names on the guest list." He opened the door and warm amber light poured onto the pavement. "After you."

Imogen stepped inside onto a black carpet. The walls were clad in wooden panels and painted a pale shade of moss green. Several photographs with glossy black frames were spotlit—each one held an image of a women tied up with intricate knotted rope.

"This way," Kane said, urging her to walk ahead of him.

Imogen moved farther into the hallway, which turned into a corridor. She was mesmerized by all of the pictures on the walls. She would have liked to stop and stare, enjoy them for a moment, but Kane was pacing behind her, as though keen to get to their destination.

A woman in a tight citrus orange dress appeared holding a clipboard. She had her hair piled on top of her head and like Imogen wore a collar, though hers had a large silver padlock hanging from it. "Ah, Master K, it is so good to see you again."

*Master K?*

"Aisha, I trust you are well," Kane said, stopping at a door with a chrome handle. He rested his hand on it.

"Very." Aisha examined Imogen through heavily lashed eyes. The kohl she'd applied licked outward to her temple in thin lines. "You've brought a guest tonight."

"Yes. She's on the list."

"I know." Aisha smiled.

Imogen didn't think the smile went high enough; it was forced, not really there, just a stretching of lips.

"Everything is in your room as requested," Aisha said, returning her attention to Kane.

"Thank you." Kane opened the door at his left.

"I guess I'll see you in there."

"Yes, though we're just observing tonight."

"No playing." Aisha appeared surprised. "What a waste of a trip." She shrugged and looked coy, sweeping her tongue over her lips.

Kane scowled. "It is what it is." His voice was harsh.

"Certainly, Sir." She dropped her gaze and stared at her feet. Hid the point of her tongue. "I'm sorry if I was impudent."

Kane said nothing; instead, he reached for Imogen's hand and steered her into what appeared to be a changing room. He shut the door and placed his bag on a table.

"You know her well?" Imogen asked.

"I've done a scene or two with her, that's all."

"A scene?" Imogen was confused. "What do you mean?"

"Played, you know…" He unbuttoned his jacket. "No,

you don't know, that was a foolish thing for me to say. I'm sorry." He paused. "But all will become clear."

"You've slept with her?" For some reason the thought made Imogen feel sick, not that it should, she had no claim on him. "I'm sorry. Don't answer that. I have no right to—"

He removed his jacket and hung it on a hook. "I haven't slept with her, that's not what being in a scene with someone means. It's very personal, very intimate, and there is a lot of different dynamics at play, trust being the big one, but there doesn't have to be sex, and there wasn't, ever, not with Aisha." He unzipped his bag. "There will be lots of things you haven't seen before once we go inside. But I don't want you to judge or take them all at face value. Beneath the surface of every act there is more going on that can't be seen."

"I don't understand."

"Just remember everything is consensual, everyone is an adult, everyone has a safe word."

Safe word—now she did know what that meant. That was if a spanking or bondage became too much. It meant stop. In the book she'd read, the heroine had a safe word—rainbow dust.

Kane withdrew a red mask from the bag. It was the same shade as the eyelets on her dress and boots.

"Here." He held it up and the two long ribbons dangled over the cuffs of his shirt. "This will ensure you remain anonymous."

"A mask?"

"Yes. It is the perfect solution, and trust me, you won't be the only one wearing a facial covering." He stepped toward her. "There are many people here who like to keep their nocturnal activities private." He paused. "Turn."

Imogen did as he'd asked. Anonymous, that suited her very well. At least until she knew what she'd gotten herself into.

As he gently placed the soft velvet over her face and tied

the ribbon at the back of her head, Imogen studied a jacket hanging on a wooden frame. It was black velvet and had three gold stars on the right shoulder. Beneath the stars was an embroidered letter K.

"Is that yours?" she asked.

"The jacket?"

"Yes."

He secured the knot. "It is."

"What are the three stars for?"

"It is a symbol of my status here."

"Which is?" Imogen pressed the mask secure; it had a tiny, flexible piece of metal set within it to mold to the shape of the bridge of her nose.

"You'll see," he said.

Imogen turned. "When?"

Kane had applied a mask, like hers, though his was gold, the same as the stitching on the jacket. "Soon." He tilted his chin and his eyes sparkled from behind thin cutouts.

He looked regal, aloof, mysterious, and so damn sexy she was sure her knickers would be soaked just from seeing him like that. The mask highlighted the sensual shape of his lips and the proud angle of his nose.

He removed his tuxedo jacket and replaced it with the velvet one; the bow tie remained in place. He brushed a speck of fluff from the sleeve. "Are you ready?"

"I'm not exactly sure what I'm meant to be ready for, but I'll give it a go."

He smiled, just a little. "Good, I knew you would. But please let yourself view the club as a newbie, a virgin if you like." He lowered his voice. "I want to know what turns you on and what turns you off. That will be essential to our trip and to the future."

Imogen's breath shivered from her throat. What turned her on was him, but it would hardly be the answer he was looking for if he wanted her opinion on décor for his new clubs.

On top of that she was intrigued to know what was

beyond these walls. What scenes she might witness, what kinks Kane might reveal. Would his kinks be hers? Not that she really knew what hers were.

"Yes, okay," she said. "But I won't have to try too hard; it likely will all be new to me."

"Yes." He paused. "So soak it all up because I will want to know, later, back at the hotel, exactly how you feel, about everything."

There was something in the way he spoke, undercurrents, that made her wonder just how deep he'd delve into her reactions. And how much would she tell him? She'd bet it would be more than just her thoughts on paint color and accessories.

Kane opened the door and they stepped out. The corridor was deserted, but Imogen could hear the distant beat of music and the hum of conversation. She could smell perfume and cologne, all mixed, and on top of that was a musky heat to the air that made her think of being hot and sweaty with a lover.

Kane reached for her hand and led the way.

Imogen glanced at the pictures on the wall. More of the same—bondage with rope weaved as intricate as lace. She was glad Kane wasn't walking fast; her boots were not designed for speed.

He paused at an archway and slipped his hand around her waist, urging her against his side.

"This is the bar area," he said. "Though few people indulge in alcohol while they're here." He gestured around. "What do you think?"

"It looks very relaxing."

And it was. Big, soft sofas were set about with low tables between them. The lighting that came from large lamps was muted, casting shadows up the walls and over the furniture. The fabrics were rich jewel colors, the paintwork and carpet black. Several people milled about near the bar, a few sat on the sofas sipping from tall glasses. Everyone was dressed in similar attire to herself and Kane.

He'd been right, she would have stood out if she hadn't taken him up on his offer of the new dress and boots. She fit right in—well, to look at anyway.

"Would you like a drink?" he asked over the sound of the music.

"I'm okay, unless you want one."

"No. I drank water after my workout." He urged her forward. "So shall we go straight into a playroom?"

"If that's what you want?"

He glanced at his watch. "There should be something going on to satisfy our voyeur plans for the evening."

They stepped toward the bar.

Kane indicated another doorway at the opposite end that had a chain mail curtain hanging from its frame. "It's through there."

"Ah, K. Long time no see." A man wearing a similar jacket to Kane's but with only two stars over the breast pocket extended his hand.

He didn't wear a mask and Imogen could see that his smile was genuine.

"Nate, how have you been?" Kane took his hand and they shook.

"Great, been in the city for a few weeks on business. Making the most of my free time by coming here." Nate turned to Imogen and raised his eyebrows. "You have company."

"Don't look so surprised." Kane squeezed Imogen a little closer.

"I am. You don't usually bring guests. Special occasion?"

Imogen felt Kane tense. She sensed he wasn't enjoying having his break from the ordinary commented on.

"No occasion," Kane said. "Good to see you, Nate, perhaps we'll get chance to catch up later."

"Yep. That would be cool." Nate held up what appeared to be a glass of fizzy water and nodded. He kept his attention on Imogen. "Enjoy your evening here at Sub Space. I'm sure Master K will address your every need."

"Thank you." Imogen smiled, then felt her cheeks heat as Nate swept his gaze down her body—starting at the collar, then lingering on her breasts and finally on her boots.

Kane stepped forward, tugging her with him. "This way."

After several paces she touched the collar. "This, around my neck," she said quietly. "What would happen if I wasn't wearing it?"

"It would make you fair bait for men like Nate, who are just out to play in a scene, find someone to hook up with." He glanced at her. "He had no right to look at you like that."

"Well, the outfit kind of screams *look at me.*"

"That's not the point."

"Oh." She was confused. "It's not?"

"No. You're with me. I've claimed you with a collar. What's more, I outrank him. He should show more respect."

"You outrank him?"

"Of course." He pulled back the chain curtain and opened a door. He ushered Imogen into the new room.

Imogen opened her mouth and stared around, thoughts of Nate vanishing.

Kane moved her from the doorway and into the shadows. He stepped behind her and wrapped his arms around her waist.

"What are your first impressions?" he asked by her ear, his lips brushing her lobe and his breath heating a trail down her neck.

She leant back into him, loving being so close and being held by him. But she couldn't concentrate fully on his embrace because of what was before her. "It's... sexy."

"Mmm, I'm glad you think so," he said, the soft material of his mask rubbing against her temple. "What else?"

She looked around. The room was sectioned into six large cubicles, each decorated in dark tones and with a combination of low lights and spotlights. Each three-walled area held a bed or a table or some other piece of equipment in the center. Three spaces were occupied.

There was an audience, too; couples, singles, threesomes sitting on more large sofas. Imogen could only see the backs of their heads. Some appeared enraptured, others holding quiet conversations.

"Tell me," Kane urged, slipping his hand over the smooth material covering her waist. "What do you think about that, over there, to your left."

Imogen was already staring in that direction. It had been the main thing that had captured her attention.

A naked woman was bent double, tied to a skinny padded table with her ankles fastened to the legs and her arms stretched out on two platforms, crucifix-like. Her skin was pale except for her behind, which was scarlet.

Beside her stood a man—dressed like Kane in black trousers and a velvet jacket—wielding a flogger. He walked around the woman as if surveying the marks on her ass, then cracked down the many strands over her skin.

Imogen jerked and a tingle traveled over her buttocks, as though her nerves were empathetic with what the woman on the table was going through.

The man hit again.

The woman groaned and moved her head, her face coming into Imogen's view. She had her eyes screwed up tight and her lips were parted. There was a flush of red on her cheeks that matched the rosy blush on her backside.

"Talk to me," Kane said softly.

"Is she enjoying it?" Imogen asked, although she was pretty sure she knew the answer. The woman appeared to be in ecstasy, as though she'd folded in on herself and only her body and sensation existed.

"Very much so," Kane said. "Master Zen is very capable of working his sub toward orgasm just through striking her."

"Are they just... playing a scene or are they...?"

"Lovers, committed to each other? Yes, actually those two are. They're regulars here and live the lifestyle."

"The lifestyle?"

"Yes." He slid his hand to her collar and spanned it with his thumb and fingers. "They live full time as dom and sub. He commands and she obeys."

"It sounds… old-fashioned." Imogen wasn't sure about the obeying thing. She'd known friends who'd purposely had that removed from their wedding vows.

"It's a symbiotic relationship," Kane went on, smoothing his fingers around her collar and brushing her skin.

A small shiver ran down Imogen's spine.

The woman was struck again—several times in fast succession.

Imogen stared at the spectacle.

"You see," Kane said. "She needs to be adored, cared for, taken through life by the man she loves. He needs to protect her, satisfy her, try his best to ensure that everything is perfect for her at all times. That is what makes him feel complete."

"And that includes this. Beating?"

"Beating, spanking, flogging, whatever you want to call it, yes, it includes this, because that's what they both enjoy, it's their thing. It's their kink."

Kane went quiet and Imogen watched as Master Zen stood directly behind his sub. He appeared to fiddle at his groin, then his pants loosened around his hips. He pushed forward.

The woman arched her back and her cry echoed around the room.

He reached for her shoulders, dragged her onto him.

"He's…" Imogen said.

"Yes. He's clearly very pleased with her. She's getting exactly what she wants tonight." Kane's voice was low and husky, as though the sight was turning him on.

Imogen watched, fascinated as the dom began to fuck his woman with urgency. The sub couldn't move, she was strapped down, but he was moving for both of them.

Thrusting in and out, hard, frantic, gripping her shoulders, her hair, her hips. His hands were all over her.

Imogen's knickers dampened and she shifted within Kane's arms.

"Would you like to get fucked like that?" Kane whispered.

Imogen half turned to him, his words a shock, despite where they were and what they were watching.

"Tell me," he said, cupping her cheek and holding her face. "Tell me what you're thinking?"

"I…" Imogen was breathing heavily. Fuck. What was she thinking? That she wanted to get fucked like that? She wanted to feel the flogger?

"Would you like to be her, on that table, with Master Zen taking you to the exquisite high she is rocketing toward right now?" Kane asked. "Red and sore, filled to the max? Nothing else in your mind except claiming that pleasure?"

She did, but it wasn't Master Zen she wanted behind her, yanking her hair, scratching and marking her skin. Sinking deep, so deep. Filling her to the bursting point.

It was Kane, or K as he was known here. It was him she wanted.

"Imogen," Kane murmured, his mouth almost touching hers. "Talk to me."

"Yes." The word scratched from her throat. "But—"

He pressed his thumb over her lips, flattening them against her teeth. "No buts. Or if there are, tell me later." He gave a brief smile. "Yes is enough."

She swallowed and nodded.

Several loud slaps rang out.

Imogen turned back to the couple who were fucking. The master had delivered hard blows with his hand to the woman's behind. She was shaking all over, her toes curled off the floor and the soles of her feet white where the blood had drained from them.

"Come," he half shouted, half growled. "You may come."

Relief seemed to vibrate over the woman then with a violent spasm; she heaved at her constraints and wailed through a climax.

Imogen was aware of a tremble of need between her legs, and her nipples spiked against the tight dress. What must it be like to be so surrendered? So absolutely under a master's control? Laid bare, everything exposed and all those raw sensations blasting around as orgasm took hold? She shivered, a pleasant tremor in her belly that extended outward and pulsed through her sex.

Kane held her a little tighter, slotting her closer.

A hard wedge of flesh jutted into her buttock.

His cock.

He was aroused too.

# CHAPTER SEVEN

Although excited by the feel of Kane's cock, Imogen brought her attention to the audience in front of her. All had paused in their conversations and were watching the scene reaching crescendo.

"Imogen," Kane whispered.

"Yes."

"Have you ever been spanked?"

"No," she said quickly. What was the point in lying?

After her rapid response he was quiet. His breaths were soft on her cheek and his chest shifted against her back. His erection continued to strain next to her buttock; she couldn't ignore it, even if the questions were demanding her concentration.

She'd never been hit by a man and until this point hoped she wouldn't be. But now? The ecstasy on that woman's face, the erotic red hue her ass had turned under her master's hand. Maybe…?

She sucked in a deep breath.

"We should sit." Kane urged her forward. "And watch something else that's new for you."

Imogen moved in the direction Kane gestured and found herself sitting on a plush purple sofa. She was glad;

her legs were a little weak. It was probably just the high heels. But she did miss feeling Kane's arousal.

She looked around—what other spectacle would there be for her to witness? She had enough to digest at the moment, and as she inched backward on the seat she was sure her ass cheeks smarted—but not in an unpleasant manner, in a way that generated the need for more.

Kane sat next to her, casually extending one arm over the back of the sofa, close but not quite touching her.

She felt surrounded by him. Protected and cocooned by his strong presence in a place where she was uninitiated and out of her depth. She knew he'd guide her through this.

A woman in a tight black trouser suit—that would have been almost decent if it weren't for circles of material missing over her breasts—came into Imogen's peripheral vision.

The femme fatale's hips swayed, and her nipples— peaked, rouged, and pierced with silver bars—jiggled as she strutted toward their purple sofa. She had a determined expression.

Kane crossed his legs, then jabbed the air with the toe of his shiny leather shoe.

The woman dropped to her knees at his feet, crumpling as though worshipping at an altar. She then bowed her head and clasped her hands behind her back, jutting her large breasts so they almost touched Kane's leg.

"Tara," Kane said, uncrossing his legs, then sitting forward in a slow, deliberate manner. He removed his arm from the back of the sofa.

"Master K," the woman said, looking up and batting her long, fake eyelashes.

"It's good to see you." Kane rested his fingertips on her shoulder.

Imogen stared at his long, dark fingers against the woman's slender frame.

She appeared to sag into his touch. Her lips parted and she raised her eyebrows, as though silently pleading.

"Not tonight." Kane shook his head.

"Please," she said, biting on her bottom lip.

"No, Tara."

"Please, I beg it of you."

"No." Kane's tone was harsher. "It is not possible."

The woman, Tara, turned to Imogen.

Imogen held her gaze. She, after all, wasn't the one on the floor, knees bent, hands in invisible shackles and breasts bared for all to see.

Although she did also have a collar around her neck.

She found herself running her finger over the lean circle of leather at her throat.

Kane reached for Imogen's other hand and linked their fingers.

"My guest and I are purely spectators tonight," he said. "So if your master would like to demonstrate the use of the St. Andrew's cross, that would be very pleasing."

"I love pleasing you," Tara said, swinging her attention back to Kane. "You know I do."

"And you do so very well on the occasions you've been required to," Kane said. "Now please, we're trying to keep a low profile."

"Yes, Sir, of course, Sir. I'm very sorry to have interrupted, Sir."

"You may go now." Kane sat back, the action dismissive to the point of rude. He added to it by flicking his fingers at Tara.

She stood, quickly, and pushed her linked fingers over her chest, flattening the soft orbs of flesh. She then backed away, head still low until she stood next to a man in a black velvet jacket who'd been watching from the shadows.

He was tall, taller than Kane, and also had three gold stars embroidered on his top. He had no hair and the skin on his scalp appeared smooth and shiny.

Tara reached his side and stood next to him, staring at her feet.

The man raised his hand to Kane.

Kane acknowledged it with a nod and resettled his arm around the back of the sofa—around Imogen.

"Is that her master?" Imogen asked.

"Yes. Master, husband, lover."

"But she...?"

"Wanted to play with me, yes." He'd preempted her question.

"But—?"

"Her master had given her permission to ask."

"And he wouldn't mind if you'd said yes?" Hell, *she* would have minded if Kane had said yes. Imogen was coping sitting here, in this... sex club. But watching Kane join in would tip her over the edge.

"No, of course not." Kane turned to her. "Why would he mind?"

"Wouldn't he be jealous?" It was the biggest emotion on Imogen's mind right now. The thought of Tara getting her ass whacked by Kane then him fucking her, here, on stage for all to see. She could think of nothing worse. If that was going to happen, then she'd want to be the woman up there on the bench.

She sucked in a breath as that certain knowledge settled into her brain. She wanted to be on that bench?

"Why would he be jealous?" Kane asked with a frown. "She loves him, they're committed to each other. Sharing a physical experience, pleasure and pain, with someone else won't change that."

"So that's not viewed as unfaithful here? To be with someone else like that?"

"No." He seemed bemused. "Not at all. It's all consensual, not just the couple in the scene but their partners too."

"So you've... with her... with him there watching...?" Imogen rubbed her hand over her brow. It was all a lot to take in. "And it didn't cause problems."

"Listen." Kane leaned forward and touched the knuckle of his finger under her chin. "Don't worry about our sexual

71

histories tonight. This is new for us to be here, spectating together. I want you to concentrate on aesthetics, the ambience, how it makes you feel as a woman. What I can do to make that experience better when I come to design my clubs."

Imogen looked into his eyes. She wanted to delve deeper. Find out what exactly was going on in that head of his. Why he'd really brought her here. Was it still about a business venture? She didn't think so, but every now and then he mentioned it, drawing her back.

"Ah, here we go," Kane said. "They're going to demonstrate the St. Andrew's cross for you. How wonderful."

"The St. Andrew's cross," Imogen repeated, staring at the sleek black structure in the cubicle before them. It was a cross on its side, so two of the bottom feet were attached to the floor creating an X shape. It had attachments that appeared to be leather cuffs near each point and soft padding in the middle. "What's it for?"

"It's one way of holding a submissive in position," Kane said, looking at Imogen and not the cross.

Tara stood before her master, head bowed as he removed her clothing. After he'd peeled the suit from her, he carefully folded it over a chair.

His lack of mask afforded Imogen a good perusal of his expression as he surveyed his naked wife. There was love there, and desire. His cheeks were a little pink and his brow furrowed with apparent concentration.

He slipped his jacket off and added it to the pile of her clothes. Then, very slowly, he slid off his tie and undid the top button of his pristine white shirt.

Tara trembled.

Imogen was pretty sure the woman's shiver wasn't from being cold, for the club was very warm. It was more likely to be anticipation, the need for the pain and pleasure to start.

When the master was ready, he led Tara to the cross. He

slid his palms over the wood as though checking for splinters or imperfections. He then raised Tara's left arm and secured it to the left angle of the cross. He did the same with the right then stooped and attached her ankles. The result of his efforts was Tara bound with her arms and legs spread and her chest pressing on the center. Her pussy lips were just visible and her ribs defined when she inhaled. Her buttocks were tight and pale, and she had a small tattoo on her lower back that looked to be Chinese writing.

"You okay?" Kane asked, slipping his hand from the sofa onto Imogen's shoulder.

"Yes." Imogen paused. "Is he going to spank her?"

"Watch."

Imogen's skin tingled between her breasts and her stomach clenched. The anticipation was making her body react and all she was doing was witnessing the act. She could hardly imagine the levels of expectancy Tara must be going through.

The master picked up what appeared to be a table tennis bat, but a little more square and with a red handle. He whacked it over his palm.

Tara jumped. The chain links on her binds rattled.

But she wasn't struck. He moved around the cubicle, surveying her. He nodded then stood in front of her. He curled one hand into her hair and kissed her hard and urgently.

Imogen crossed and uncrossed her legs. She licked her lips.

Tara's master moved to one of the locker units in the cubicle. He pulled open a drawer and slipped something into his trouser pocket.

After another slap of the paddle on his palm, he moved behind Tara.

This was it.

Imogen's mouth was dry. She wished she had a drink of water.

What must Tara be feeling right now? Waiting for that

first slice of pain. That first strike.

The *thwack* of the paddle caught the audience's attention. Everyone spun to see Tara yank her arms and legs and jerk against the cross.

"The paddle delivers a hard sting," Kane said quietly. "It makes the outer nerves smart and then works its way down to the deeper ones to give a bruising sensation, like a deep massage."

Imogen didn't reply. She couldn't imagine what it must feel like.

Tara was hit again, the opposite buttock this time. She flung her head back and arched her spine. The skin on her rear rippled and shook.

Several more hits rained down, all landing on the roundest sections of her ass cheeks and creating ear-splitting cracks that echoed around the quiet room.

After a few minutes, and when Tara's skin glowed ruby red, her master set down the paddle. He kneeled behind her and, spreading his fingers wide, he caressed her thighs, her buttocks, and her lower back. It was as though he was admiring his handiwork and was fascinated by the results.

Tara sagged, allowing the cross to hold her.

Imogen's heart was beating fast. She pushed a stray lock of hair behind her ear and wondered what was going to happen next.

Tara's master pulled something from his pocket.

Imogen tipped her head to try to see around him, get a glimpse of what it was.

Kane's arm shifted on her shoulder. He ran his hand to her neck and stroked the collar.

Imogen glanced at him.

He was staring straight at her.

"Are you okay?" he asked quietly. "With this?"

"The collar?"

He smiled, just a little. "It suits you. What I meant was watching this scene. It's not over yet."

The collar suited her? "Er, yes. I'm fine."

"It's what she wants."

Imogen nodded and tore her gaze from Kane. She didn't know what was happening now, but Tara's master was busy behind her on his hands and knees.

"What's happening?" Imogen asked quietly.

"He's inserting a butt plug."

"A butt plug?" Imogen turned to Kane, her eyes wide.

"It's what she wants. It's what she likes."

"Oh…" Damn. Imogen wished she didn't seem so naive but she'd never used or even seen a butt plug before. Yet here she was, witnessing one being inserted.

"Anal play is common here," Kane said, moving his finger from the collar to the base of Imogen's neck. "The sensations add to the experience."

Tara groaned and let her head fall back, so that she was gazing at the ceiling. Her long dark hair swayed down her spine, swishing over her skin. Her fists were clenched and when one groan ended, another began.

It certainly seemed like the butt plug was enhancing Tara's experience.

Her master stood. He picked up the paddle and slapped each of Tara's buttocks hard and fast.

Tara cried out. Her ass clenched.

"See now, when he hits, she can't help but react by contracting her internal muscles," Kane said. "That means the plug will press on all those little sweet spots high inside. She'll want to come really soon."

"Oh, God," Imogen murmured. She'd found that she'd clenched her own buttocks, her pussy muscles too.

Kane slid his finger from her nape across to her shoulder, the one nearest him. He drew a circle then stroked down her arm.

A shiver of longing went through Imogen. She wasn't sure exactly what she was longing for, but Kane was definitely at the heart of the need building in her.

Tara's master moved to the front of the cross.

Imogen could see his face now. A slick of sweat sat on

his hairless head and his lips were pressed tight, as though he was determined in his mission.

He kissed Tara again, hard, and delved one hand between her legs.

Tara bucked and writhed but couldn't move far. Her skin glowed and when she arched her back, the base of the plug, a large sapphire jewel, was visible.

"Now what's happening?" Imogen asked.

Kane leaned a little closer. "He's going to make her come."

His breath washed over Imogen's shoulder and seemed to trickle down to her nipples.

Damn, she was so turned on just watching this. She'd never thought she would be. But Kane at her side—not businesslike, efficient Kane, but seductive, mysterious, sexy Kane—had her wanting sex in a way she never had before.

She swallowed, resisted squirming, and blew out a breath through pursed lips.

The master was working his sub with his hand, fingering her and stimulating her clit.

"More, more, please, Sir," Tara cried.

Her master reached behind her, gripped her poor marked ass and squeezed.

She howled and thrust forward then backward. "Yes, yes." Her body trembled and shook. A glistening moisture appeared between her legs as she came.

"Oh…" Imogen said on a sigh.

Kane placed his hand on her cheek and turned her to face him. He didn't speak, just stared into her eyes.

Imogen blinked rapidly. The whoosh of her pulse in her ears swirled with Tara's cries of release.

Kane frowned, his lips a tight straight line.

Imogen felt as though he was looking into her soul, into the very heart of her desires. In that moment, she didn't think she could hide anything from him.

She didn't want to.

She'd just learned that she wanted more, that she

wouldn't be satisfied until she'd explored why watching a flogging and a spanking had turned her on so much. The need to know how it would feel to have Kane strap her down and make her come was almost overwhelming.

"Good girl," he said. "That's it. Embrace it."

"Embrace what?"

"Every aspect of your sexuality. It is the only true way to exist."

She nodded.

"I didn't make a mistake bringing you here, did I?"

"No."

"You understand what you've seen?"

"Not all of it, but I want to know more."

"You're curious?"

"Yes."

"Then we have achieved what I hoped we would tonight."

"We have?"

"Absolutely." He released her face and glanced at his watch. "We should go now. That's enough for your first visit."

# CHAPTER EIGHT

The hotel suite was silent as Imogen stepped in. She paused and watched Kane remove his tuxedo jacket and rest it on the back of the sofa. He'd changed from the black velvet one as they'd left the club, explaining that it was Sub Space rules that gold star jackets remained on the premises.

She glanced toward her bedroom, then over at the room Kane had used to shower and change. The place was so huge, so extravagant, but right now she'd happily be in a small, standard room with only one bed so there'd be no question about them sharing. Because if she didn't get some relief soon from the frustration growing deep in her belly she was sure she'd go mad.

All the way back in the limo she'd thought about what she'd seen—the spanking, the pale female skin turning red, the men pleasing their women, mastering them, wringing sublime orgasms from them.

She imagined Kane there. In that role. Performing, satisfying his urges, sating his desires. But she didn't think of the women he was with, she only saw herself there, bent over for him, legs spread for him, her arms reaching for him.

She kept her focus on him now as he turned up the cuffs on his shirt, three neat rolls on each sleeve. He did it in that controlled way of moving he had, unhurried, very precise. The low lights created heavy shadows on his features and in the vertical creases on his shirt. Behind him, through the huge windows, New York twinkled and seemed to create a glow for him to bask in. Halo-like—but she now knew that he was no angel.

Imogen shifted on her heels. Her feet were aching a little. The flesh between her legs was aching a lot.

"Please, allow me," Kane said. He dropped to one knee.

"Kane?"

He took her left foot in his hand. "Your feet are starting to complain, I'm sure. These boots are new."

"Er, yes." Imogen rested her hand on his shoulder, absorbing the hardness of his body beneath the material of his shirt. "A bit."

Very gently, Kane wriggled the shoe section of the boot then slowly, oh so slowly, slid it off, revealing her leg. Once that boot was set aside, he repeated the process with the other one.

He stood, uncurling his spine and smoothing the material at his groin.

Imogen watched him straighten. He was once again taller than her and she felt small in her bare feet next to him.

"I'm sure the senior partners at Coutts would have a fit to see one of their most valued clients on his knees removing my boots," she said.

"Coutts' senior partners are a million miles away," Kane said. He reached behind his neck and undid his bow tie. It slid from beneath the collar and he tossed it aside so it landed next to his jacket.

"Yes, I suppose they are."

"Everyone and everything is a million miles away." He spoke in a low, husky whisper. "There's only us, Imogen. Nothing else exists at this moment in time."

"I like that thought." She pulled in a deep breath. The dress suddenly felt tight and restrictive. "I like it a lot."

"It's that blankness many subs strive for," he said,

glancing at her breasts as they pushed forward with her breaths, the lace of the corset straining. "They enjoy letting go of all responsibility, and only the physical existing. Real life worries fade away. It's a break from normality and the daily grind. It's a place that calls to them."

Imogen remembered the willing surrender of the women at the club, at the total lack of control and the awe-inspiring trust they had in the men playing their bodies like fine instruments. "I think I can understand that now." She reached for her collar. Standing so close to Kane with him looking at her with such intensity was making her hot, as was thinking of the club. She had the urge to fidget, though didn't dare risk breaking the spell.

"Please," he said. "Leave that on. For a little while longer."

"The collar?"

"Yes."

"Okay." She took hold of the top bow that held the front of her outfit together. He wanted the collar on, but would he object to her removing the dress? She didn't think so, but she couldn't be sure—predictability didn't go on Kane Ward's résumé.

But she'd take the chance. For the sake of her sanity, she'd offer him what she thought he wanted, hoped he needed. Even if it meant her ass cheeks got a beating— which didn't sound like a wholly unpleasant option, even if it was a bit scary.

She tugged and the ribbon slid free.

Kane shut his eyes. His lashes cast shadows on his cheeks.

For a few seconds she thought he would stay that way but then he opened his eyes and stared straight at her. He tipped his chin upward. His expression was stern.

Her heart rate skittered, but Imogen continued to pull the lace, threading it through the eyelets. The dress relaxed around her breasts, and air washed over her cleavage as it was revealed.

"Imogen," Kane said breathily, with a slight frown marring his brow.

"What?" she asked. Damn, was she reading this all wrong? Well, it was too late now, the dress was coming off. Another few tugs and the straps would slip down her arms and it would pool at the floor around her feet.

"I want you," he said hoarsely.

*He did. Thank God.*

"And I want you." She paused. "And if you need to bend me over, tie me up, hit my backside to get off, then I'm willing to try it." She would, right now, for him. If it was what he needed.

He reached for her face, his fingers gentle on her cheeks. "Baby," he whispered, his lips hovering over hers. "I have my kinks, no doubt about that, but not tonight. Not this first time with you."

She held onto his forearms.

He was tense, the muscles and tendons taut and sinewy.

"But I thought—" she started.

"You thought wrong." He touched his mouth to hers. It was a gentle, respectful kiss, no tongue, just lips pressing together. He pulled back a fraction and stared into her eyes.

"I did." She curled her toes on the carpet and was aware of the dress slipping until the straps caught halfway down her upper arms. "I thought wrong?"

"Yes. Because sometimes…" He glanced downward, at her breasts partly exposed now by the gape in her outfit.

"Because what?"

"Because sometimes vanilla is the best flavor." He slid his touch from her face to her shoulders, then to her arms. "Sometimes vanilla is the only flavor that will do, Imogen."

"Vanilla?"

"No spanking, no bondage. Just us."

She let out a breath she hadn't known had trapped itself in her throat. "Okay." She could handle that. Maybe it would be for the best. This time at least.

She released his arms and allowed the straps to fall. The

entire dress landed on the floor. She kicked it aside, aware of her naked breasts swaying as she moved.

He rubbed the tip of his finger over his left eyebrow and stared down at her. He pressed his teeth into his bottom lip.

Imogen forced herself still. All the times she'd fantasized about Kane she'd never envisioned this moment. Wearing nothing but a pair of tiny black knickers in a top-class suite in New York hadn't entered her imagination. Nor had the thought that he'd be into bondage and floggers.

Yet now it couldn't be more perfect.

"You're beautiful," he said. "Even more so than I thought possible."

Her nipples were tight, hard peaks and the tiny hairs on her arms prickled. A warmth went through her at his words—he thought she was beautiful.

"Turn around," he said.

She did as he'd asked. Her line of sight settled on a huge bunch of lilac and cream flowers on a dresser.

"So perfect," he said quietly. "Your skin. It's flawless." He cupped her buttocks. His hands were big and hot and his fingertips sank into the lower curve.

He came closer, his chest touching her back as he drifted his hands over the waistband of her knickers. "Give me strength," he murmured against the angle of her neck.

"For what?" she asked, reaching up and resting her hand on his stubbled cheek.

"To not take you to the edge tonight."

"Do whatever you want to me, Kane." Had she really just said that? To a master from Sub Space. Was she insane?

"I think you should retract that offer immediately." He kissed her neck, then gave it a sharp bite.

"Ow." She jumped within his arms.

"Shh, just be careful what you say to me. I'm a mere mortal after all."

She wriggled a little within his hold and his erection strained at the top rise of her buttocks. "But maybe I could handle it."

"Maybe you could, maybe you couldn't. But tonight is not about that, it's about us." He kissed down her neck and slipped his caress up her stomach to her breasts. He held their weighty underside and flicked his thumbs over her nipples. "This has been too long a wait."

Imogen groaned and pressed her palms over his knuckles. She'd been on the edge for what felt like hours and now she needed more, so much more. "I agree, it's been a long day."

"I'm not talking about today." He kissed up her neck, to the shell of her ear.

"You're not?"

"No, I've been waiting for this for months. Waiting to get my hands on you, touch you, learn everything about you."

She shut her eyes and let those words settle. Damn, it was exactly how she felt too. "Kane."

"Yes?"

"Fuck me."

He chuckled and grazed his teeth over her earlobe. "I always knew there was a bad girl in there."

"Yes, well, I think you've tempted her out to play." Her voice was breathy.

Suddenly he spun her to face him.

She gasped. Her chest mashed against his shirt and his cock strained at her belly as he pulled her close.

"Be careful, baby, you're playing with a dom." He rammed his mouth down on hers. His tongue probed between her lips, and as he slanted his head to get a better angle it went deeper, sweeping into her mouth.

Imogen clung to his shoulders and gave as good as she got. She'd been waiting so long for this kiss. This hot, hard, desperate kiss with Kane. The man of her fantasies, the man who was now holding her as if he would never let go.

He stooped and cupped her ass.

Imogen was lifted into the air. Instinctively, she wrapped her legs around his waist and her arms about his neck. She clung to him. Their kiss didn't break as he strode toward her bedroom.

The thin strip of material covering her pussy was damp and pressing onto Kane's clothing. She wanted him naked. So many times she'd imagined his bare torso, and now here she was with barely a stitch on and he was fully dressed. She reached for the top fastened button on his shirt and one-handedly undid it. Time to rectify the situation.

He kept on walking as she undid the next and the next. Once in the bedroom, he tipped her onto the bed. He hovered over her, trapped by her legs still curled about his waist. She pulled at the material on his shirt and yanked it from the waistband of his trousers. With another tug she had it up his back and sliding over his head.

Finally she had a chance to admire Kane's body. Even though the room was in semi-darkness, she could see that his skin was tanned and his pecs and abs defined. He had a good coating of body hair, which she'd expected as he was so dark and his facial stubble so thick. What she hadn't expected were three small tattoos just below his right collarbone—small stars, like the ones on his jacket at the club.

She slid her hands over him, caught his nipples beneath her fingers, then smoothed round to his shoulders.

He released a small moan. "Imogen."

"Mmm?"

"While I still have some rational thought in my head, I should ask…" He paused and looked down at her breasts.

"What?"

"Should I? Do I need to wear a condom?" He glanced back up at her face. "I'm clean."

It hadn't been what she'd been expecting him to ask. She let her legs slip from the tight grip she had on his waist. "I, er… no. I had a full check a few months ago."

"And…" He pressed his groin against her pussy and the hard length of his cock rubbed over her panties. "Are we in danger of making any little Kanes and Imogens?" His lips twitched, as if he were holding in a smile.

She caught her breath. "No, no, that's covered. Pill." But damn, the thought of having his babies...

"In that case, we should get this show on the road."

"Yes, take the bull by the horns," she added.

"Excellent analogy." He dropped his head and kissed her. As he did so, he maneuvered them both up the bed until her head was on the pillow.

Imogen ran her hands over his buttocks, touching him through his trousers. Damn, why was he still wearing clothes? "Take these off," she said. "Now."

"Bossy little thing, aren't you," he said, ducking and taking her right nipple into his mouth. He massaged her other breast, tweaking and teasing, scooping the flesh into his palm.

Imogen shut her eyes and ran her hands over his hair. So many times she'd dreamed of touching him, having him touch her, and now it was happening.

He spread his kisses downward, over her navel and to her lower abdomen, his hands spanning her waist, his thumbs stroking her skin.

She fisted the sheet and watched as he kissed her mound over her panties. He lingered and breathed deep, as though taking in her aroused scent.

"Kane..."

"You have no idea what you do to me," he said, slipping his fingers into the elastic of her underwear. "Or how difficult this is for me."

"What do you mean?"

"To fuck. I just want to fuck. Take you to places you haven't been before."

"So do it. Take me."

He shut his eyes for a moment and shook his head. "Give me strength." He pulled at her knickers, exposing her thin strip of pubic hair and her pussy.

He moved quickly and efficiently, tugged them over her feet, then stood from the bed.

He loomed large through the shadows. He was breathing fast, his wide shoulders shifting up and down. He reached for his belt buckle and undid it, slowly drawing the leather through the loops.

She swallowed and watched it slide free.

He twisted the buckle end around his fist, twice.

Imogen stared at the leather held tight in his hand and the dangling strip that hung down past his knee. Damn, that looked like a pretty good flogging implement.

*Is that what he's going to do?*

She clenched her buttocks. Butterflies of nerves alighted in her stomach. He'd said vanilla—had he changed his mind? Was he going to make her ass red and sore, then fuck her?

He was staring at her, just staring at her.

She felt sacrificial, vulnerable... she felt like his.

"Damn it," he muttered, dropping the belt suddenly. He undid his fly and his trousers loosened. He pushed them off, then slipped his black boxer briefs down his legs.

Imogen wished the lights in the room were on, that she had more than just the glow from the New York skyline. She wanted to see him, all of him.

He stepped to the side of the bed, and she saw his cock in silhouette, jutting up and out from a mass of groin hair.

Fuck, the guy was big, but again, she'd expected that.

As if guessing her thoughts about light, he flicked on the side lamp. A warm radiance filled the room.

"I need to see you," he said, climbing onto the bed next to her. "Every bit of you."

Imogen nodded and reached for him. She dragged his warm body close and breathed in the scent of his skin.

He kissed her, his cock nudging against her hip as he stroked her upper body. "I need to know," he murmured, "what you liked and didn't like at the club."

"Is this business talk?" She pulled back and traced her finger over his jawline. "You want to know if I liked the color of the walls?"

"No," he growled. "I want to know what turned you on. Made you wet…" His caress traveled to her pussy. "Here." He dipped his finger between her lips and pressed her clit, just lightly.

"Mmm…" Imogen said, "*that* turns me on."

"I mean the spanking you saw. How did that make you feel?" He spoke onto her cheek, then kissed up to her temple.

"Hot, sexy, I… liked it."

He eased through her pussy and found her entrance.

Imogen spread her legs wider, wanting to feel him there, needing penetration. "Oh…" she said on a sigh. "Yes… more…"

"Talk and I'll give you more."

Talk, yes, she could do that. "I liked watching the flogging, the woman on the bench, that turned me on. Seeing her strapped down, fucked like that."

"At the club you said *but*. I asked if you'd like to be that woman and you said yes *but*…" He smoothed around her pussy, teasing by not going near her clit or inside her.

"But." Fuck, she struggled to remember now. Kane touching her was pretty distracting. She shifted her hips, hoping for more.

"What was the but…?" he asked against her ear. "Tell me, but what?"

Ah, now she recalled the words that had been in her head. "But, but I wanted it to be you, Kane, not Master Zen behind me, flogging me, fucking me. I would only do that with you."

"Oh, perfect answer." He pushed into her—two long, firm fingers.

Imogen moaned and clenched her internal muscles around the invasion.

"Jesus, you're so hot and tight," he said, propping onto his elbow and looking down at her.

"And you've got me ready to beg for it," she managed, reaching for his cock. It was time to get serious.

"Ah, ah, ah…" He shifted away and gave a devilish grin. "Not yet, you must tell me more."

"About what?" She pouted.

"The club." He withdrew from her pussy then pushed back in, a slow finger fuck.

Imogen gripped his forearm and felt his muscles tense beneath the skin as he moved. Damn, the guy was hot, a tease for sure, but really hot.

"Tell me about the cross," he said. "Would you like to be tied to that with me paddling your sexy ass until it's red and sore?"

"Yes. Yes, I'd try it." Just the thought sent more moisture to her pussy.

The heel of his hand connected with her clit and produced the dense pressure she'd been craving.

She moaned and clutched him tighter.

"And the butt plug?" he said. "Have you ever tried one?"

"No… never."

He set up a steady rhythm, in and out of her pussy, riding over her clit. An orgasm was buried deep, but his ministrations were tempting it to the surface. She groaned and squirmed; the soft, moist sounds of him easing into her dampness turned her on all the more.

"So you're an anal virgin?" he whispered.

"Er, yes, I suppose so." She'd never really thought about anal sex. Never been with anyone who'd suggested trying it.

"How delicious," he whispered. "To have all that pleasure to come."

"I—"

"What about bondage?" he asked, upping the pace of his hand.

"Oh, God." Imogen tensed her thighs and closed her eyes. He was getting it just right, mounting up the pressure.

"Imogen," he said sternly. "Bondage. You ever been tied up?"

"Er, no, I mean, yes, once, with a scarf, messing about… not like that…" She paused. An orgasm was approaching.

"Not like what?"

"So seriously, ropes, benches… ah… fuck, I'm going to…"

"You've never been strapped down with ropes and handcuffs."

"No, no… I, God, please, I'm coming…"

"Yes, you may come, come now." He ratcheted it up a level, fingering her G-spot and rubbing her clit. "Come, baby. I need to see you come."

"I'm coming now." She opened her eyes and stared up at him.

He was looking at her with wild intensity, his shoulder shifting as he pumped his fingers into her hard and fast.

Her abdomen tensed and she curled forward, pressing onto him. She gasped as release overtook her. She dug her fingernails into his forearm as pleasure shot from her pussy. Her skin tingled, her cunt spasmed. Still he kept on dragging out her bliss.

"So fucking beautiful," he said. "I knew you would be."

"Oh… Kane…" She pushed at his hand—it was so much, too much. "That's it, please. I need to catch… my breath."

He slipped his hand from her and she flopped backward and drew her legs together. Aftershocks rippled through her pussy and she moaned with each one.

He caught her face in his damp hand and kissed her, his stubble catching on her chin.

After a moment she pulled back. "You play dirty," she said, smiling.

"What? Me?" He tweaked her right nipple and drew it to a point.

"Yes, you, Mr. Ward."

He smiled. "I just have ways and means of getting what I want."

"And you wanted to find out about my sexual experience to date."

"I've only just scratched the surface of what I want to

find out about you, and only just started on the experiences I want to give you." He leaned down and took her nipple between his teeth. He bit gently then tugged, pulling it to a long, stretched point.

Imogen let out a juddering sigh; the discomfort held dark pleasure. She wanted him to stop, but wanted more.

Kane released her nipple, then applied the same treatment to the other one.

Again she tensed at the pain, but then relaxed into it, let it spread over her breast.

He stopped and a slow smile tugged his lips wide. "It's time to fuck," he said.

"Yes." Her heart was beating wildly—she was desperate to feel him inside her.

She reached for him as he slid over her, his body weight pressing into her slightly. He was all she could see, smell, feel. Had she ever been so overtaken by a man before?

His cock nudged up against her entrance and she spread her legs wider.

"I want you to come again," he said, his lips brushing hers as he spoke. "I want to feel you come around my dick."

"Yes, Kane, please…" She wriggled a little, pushing herself onto his smooth cockhead.

He groaned and curled his hips under—entered her an inch.

She gasped. Fuck, he was wide and it had been a while.

He took her some more, kissed her at the same time, his tongue probing the way his cock was.

Imogen shut her eyes and became lost in him. She allowed her pussy to relax as he slipped through her wetness, stretching her and filling her.

"Oh, sweet Jesus," he murmured when he hit full depth. "You have no idea how many times I've wanted to be buried balls deep in you." He paused and smoothed her hair from her forehead. "When I've seen you in meetings in those tight skirts, hair all neat, fuck, I've just wanted to mess you up, make you dirty, make you and your cunt mine."

His uncharacteristically crass words turned her on even more.

He pulled out then eased back in, covering her clit in hard pressure. "Mmm…" he said on an outward breath, his eyes closing for a moment. "Fucking yeah…"

Imogen wrapped her legs around his waist again, tipped her hips to meet him and felt his cock drive even deeper— the tip pressing on her cervix and creating a deep, dense sensation. She didn't usually come more than once when having sex, but she was pretty sure it was about to happen. She felt so alive, so at one with him. His desire was electric and his body everything hers needed.

She had a sudden urge to see him, be on top. She shoved at his shoulder and twisted her body.

He fell to the side, a look of surprise on his face, as she went with him, taking the lead.

Without dislodging him from her pussy, Imogen sat astride his hips, with her back straight and breasts jutting forward.

He reached for her nipples, rolled them between his fingers and gave a low chuckle. "You've a lot to learn, little lady."

"I'm sure I have." She wasn't too sure what he was referring to, but at that moment all she could think of was how deep his cock was. This new angle had seemingly lodged him higher still, and the sensation tightened her throat and made her skin prickle. She wanted to come again.

She rocked her hips, rubbing her clit onto him. She did it again, and again, picking up speed.

He was staring up at her, his eyes wide, his lips slightly parted.

"Oh, fuck, I'm going to…" she said, tipping her head to the ceiling and shutting her eyes. She flailed her arms as the pressure built.

He caught her hands and linked their fingers. "Yes, come again, let it take you."

She gripped him, holding on as she picked up the pace,

racing for a climax that she had complete control over. She held her breath; it was there, one more...

"Ah... yeah..." she said, bliss spilling over her body and pounding through her pussy.

Suddenly she was in his arms—he'd sat forward and encased her. He shoved his hips upward and buried his face in her neck.

He grunted and dragged her down onto his cock, several hard connections that pushed air from her lungs.

"That's it..." he said breathlessly, cradling the back of her head and forcing her to look at him. "That's... fucking... it." He jerked his hips again, pulled back his lips and wrinkled his nose.

More orgasmic spasms tugged at her pelvis as she was aware of him coming inside her. She kissed him, hard, rode through the ecstasy with him. He was hot, his breaths fast, and his biceps held her pincer-like in his embrace.

In one swift move she was beneath him again.

He thrust into her, a tremor besieging him.

"That was... worth the wait," she said, kissing his cheek.

He drifted his caress down her waist to her thigh, hooked his hand beneath it and pulled her leg up. "Every bit of you has been worth waiting for."

"I'm glad you think so."

"I do." He withdrew, then pushed back in, sliding through the wetness.

Imogen moaned; she wanted it again. More. Not that she wasn't satisfied, she was; she just wasn't sure if she'd ever get enough of Kane Ward. A tremble traveled over her body. He was so edgy and they'd only just started. Where would this journey take her with this man who was both commanding and demanding? One thing she was sure of, he'd take her to places she hadn't been before, and that knowledge was both thrilling and frightening.

# CHAPTER NINE

"I'm afraid I have back-to-back meetings this morning," Kane said, straightening his navy tie.

"That's okay." Imogen propped onto her elbow and watched him. He was so handsome in a black suit that fitted him to perfection and a pale blue shirt. She couldn't imagine anyone in any meeting not going along with what he said. He held such an air of authority, of competence and power.

As he turned to face her, she swished her legs beneath the duvet, enjoying the feel of the sheets on her naked skin.

"I really would rather be with you." He walked up to the bed and took his wallet from his inner jacket pocket.

"And I'd rather be with you," she said with a smile, thinking how wonderful it had been to wake up in his arms. "But you've got an empire to run."

He gave a small shrug. "It's just work."

"It's important."

"So are you." He leaned down and pressed a kiss to her forehead. "Here." He flipped open his wallet and retrieved a golden credit card. "Go shopping."

Imogen stared at the card. He wanted to give her money, for shopping?

"Buy another outfit for Sub Space," he said. "I'd like to

take you back there." He offered the card forward. "Tonight if I can organize it."

"But—"

"And a dress for dinner. I'd like us to meet up with my brother Taylor tomorrow night. The pin number for this card is one, two, three."

"I have a dress for dinner." Imogen didn't take the card; instead, she sat and the covers slipped to her waist.

Kane glanced at her breasts. "Okay, well, buy what you want. A new handbag, shoes, whatever it is you'd like to treat yourself to." He put the card on the bed, then quickly checked his watch. "I have to go. I'll be back at four. Please be here."

She could feel a flush rising up her chest to her cheeks, but it wasn't a blush, it was irritation—extreme irritation. She didn't want his credit card. Suddenly the collar she'd slept in felt tight and restricting. Quickly, she undid it and set it aside.

"Four," he said, walking toward the door.

"No." She shoved at the covers and stood. "Wait right there."

He stopped. Turned. A frown ran across his brow as he took in her bare neck.

"I don't want this." She picked up the card and strode naked up to him. She held it between them. "I don't want your money to go shopping. I have my own money."

"But I have more and I've told you what I want you to buy." He seemed genuinely confused and also a bit peeved.

She paused. "I know you have more money, few people on the planet do have more than you, but still, I work hard so I have cash for nice things. I don't need you to spend money on me. I'm grateful for the trip and the hotel and the leather dress, but please…" She waggled the card. "I can shop with my own money."

"But I want you to have mine." He took a step back and folded his arms. His jacket bunched and his tie wrinkled.

"Don't you see?" Imogen said.

"No. I don't see." He shook his head.

"I'm used to taking care of myself, Kane. I'm independent."

"And I adore that about you."

"So don't take it away."

He unfolded his arms. "I'm not, I just don't agree with you spending your own money on things I've asked you to purchase, or as a way to pass the time because I can't be with you."

"Well, we'll have to agree to disagree. Whatever this is, between us, money is not part of the equation."

"Money is always part of the equation." He said it as though fact and non-negotiable.

"That's where you're wrong."

He raised his eyebrows.

Imogen got the feeling Kane Ward wasn't told he was wrong very often. She quickly carried on. "Money is important, yes, but not between two people who are..." She struggled to find the words. What the hell was this they were doing?

"What. Two people who are what...?" he asked quietly, his eyes narrowed.

"I don't know, two people who are attracted to each other." She gestured to the bed. "Sleeping together. Money isn't a factor, not for me at least."

"That's not been my experience with women in the past."

"I'm sure it hasn't been." She softened her voice and slipped the card into his jacket pocket. "But I'm different."

He stared at her, his gaze seeming to penetrate right through her, even more so because she was naked and he was fully clothed.

But she kept her shoulders back, stood tall. She'd worked too long to become the woman she was; she wouldn't back down from her pride in being self-sufficient.

"You certainly are different," he said. "Very different." He stepped back and touched the knot of his tie, straightened his jacket. "I have to go. I'll see you later."

Imogen watched as he left the room, shutting the door behind him.

Silence enveloped her and she was left with the image of his dark expression.

For goodness' sake, had he really thought she'd jump at the chance to go shopping on him? The idea was so alien to her. How could she spend someone else's cash like that? Not to mention there was something uncomfortable about spending the night with a man and then being given money the next morning. That really didn't sit well with her.

No, she'd much rather give her own bank balance a bashing on Fifth Avenue than Kane Ward's, even if, like he'd said, he had more than her.

Not wanting to get back into bed now that she was up and feeling twitchy, Imogen wandered into the huge bathroom and turned on the shower.

New York sprawled into the distance, and as she stood in the cubicle shampooing her hair, she could still see a few rooftops piercing a bright blue sky. She'd get dressed and go shopping as he'd suggested, yes, perhaps even for some clothes for the club, though she wasn't sure what shops sold them. And as for a dress for dinner, she had the perfectly nice one she'd brought with her. She wouldn't buy handbags and shoes as he'd suggested, but she would shop for a few gifts, for her mother and for Clarris and Katie. It would be fun to explore the city's shops, maybe get lunch out.

But she'd be back by four o'clock. No point in missing out on time with Kane, even if there likely would be more talk about money.

• • • • • • •

Three hours later and Imogen had purchased several gifts and enjoyed a coffee and a sandwich in a busy Starbucks. The streets and shops were bustling, the sun was shining. She enjoyed the ambience, the feeling that she was in the hub of the action, the place to be.

She lingered in Victoria's Secret, wandering around the section that had pretty matching bra and knickers. She thought of the dress she'd worn to the club, the one with the corset-style front. It had been super-sexy to wear and clearly Kane had liked it.

A black lace basque caught her attention. It was almost see-through, the lace was so delicate, and the bra cups were neat and molded. It had suspender elastic sewn into it and a pair of matching knickers.

Imogen picked up her size. It was incredibly pretty and sexy. Perhaps she'd get stockings to go with it and wear it beneath the black dress when they went for dinner. Kane would get a treat back at the suite if he undressed her.

Joy seeped through her. Just yesterday she wouldn't have dared have such hopes for her and Kane, yet now, after just one night—one amazing, new, kinky night—it was all she could think about.

Quickly, she went to the till to purchase the outfit, grabbing a pair of stockings from a rack on the way. Having a man in her life to show off nice underwear to was a pleasure that had been absent for too long.

"This is so gorgeous," the sales assistant said. There was no one else at the single till tucked next to the nightgown section.

"Yes, it really is very beautiful."

"Oh, are you from England?"

"Yes, London." Imogen nodded and looked at the girl's pretty blue eyes.

"I'd love to go there. It's a dream of mine."

"Well, it's pretty special to come here for me."

She rang up the goods and placed them in a bag. "What sights have you seen?"

"Not much yet." *Apart from a sex club.* "I only arrived yesterday." Imogen handed over her debit card.

"Well, Fifth Avenue is a good place to start."

"Yes, it is."

The girl nodded as she waited for the card to connect. "Are you just clothes shopping?"

"And a few gifts." Imogen thought of the dress she'd worn to the club. She had no idea where to buy something like that in New York. "And a dress. For a night out."

"Oh, dinner? Broadway?"

"No, not quite." Imogen glanced around then looked at the shop assistant again. What the hell? She had nothing to lose. "I need a dress for a club."

"Okay." She passed Imogen her card back. "A night club?"

"Kind of but…something a bit different, really sexy, kinky sexy."

She nodded, twice, long and slow. "Kinky sexy. Mmm…"

"Do you know where I could get something like that? Within walking distance of here."

The assistant glanced around. "Actually I do. If you go out of here and turn left at the next block, follow until you reach Fourth then take a right…" She paused. "Yes, take a right and then there's a smaller back street, heads uptown. Along there's a shop called Stepping Out. It has some really cool stuff, edgy, you know. Not the sort of clothes you'd rock up to your parents' anniversary party in."

"That sounds perfect."

"Shouldn't take more than ten minutes to walk."

"Thank you. You're a star. I'll head there now."

She grinned and her eyes sparkled. "Have fun."

"Oh, I think I will."

Imogen took the bag and left Victoria's Secret feeling like she was on a mission. A fetish dress was within reach—she could hardly wait.

She followed the shop assistant's directions exactly and became aware, as she turned that last corner, that she was in the street Kane had brought her to the night before. The discreet entrance to Sub Space was just a few doors along. It gave her hope that she'd find exactly what she was looking for in Stepping Out.

She paused in front of the shop. It had one large window with a single mannequin wearing a tight black all-in-one outfit that included a hood with the eyes cut out. The door was set in a recess and had an *open* sign hanging from a hook on the inside.

Imogen stepped in.

The scent of incense laced her tongue and she paused as her eyes adjusted to the light. The products were spotlit but the place itself was dim. Music played quietly, something slow and in French.

"Hey there."

Imogen spotted a young woman sitting behind a till. She recognized her: Tara, the woman who'd sat at Kane's feet the night before, then been spread-eagled on the cross and brought to climax by her master.

For a moment Imogen faltered. She wondered if she should say hello, then remembered that she wouldn't be recognized, she'd been wearing a mask. "Good afternoon," she said.

"Can I help you with anything?"

"Er, yes, I think so. I'm looking for a dress."

"Any particular material? We have leather, PVC, lace…"

Imogen took in her surroundings. The mannequin in the window was visible; the black chiffon curtain hanging behind it was almost transparent because of the light outside. "Actually, maybe an all-in-one if you have one; leather, I think."

"Yes, you look a size four, is that right?"

"Well, in UK I'm a ten, is that the same?"

Tara stood and set down the nail file she'd been holding. "That's a six, and yes, we've got a few to choose from."

Imogen walked with her to a long rail of all-in-one outfits.

"Do you want crotchless?"

Crotchless? Imogen hadn't thought about that. It would be good for access, yes, but she wasn't quite ready to walk around a club like that. "No, I don't think so."

"This one is nice." Tara pulled a black all-in-one suit from a rail. It had a high collar, long sleeves, and a silver zipper that ran from the top right to the crotch. She spun it around and showed that the zipper went right up the cleft of the buttocks too, so that plenty of body could be exposed. "It's very popular."

"It's... lovely." Imogen meant it; there was something about it...

"And these zips," Tara said, fingering one of the two zippers that were curved like breasts, "are great if you're going to start playing with nipple clamps or something like that." She undid one, showing Imogen that a woman's breasts would indeed be accessible.

Would Kane like it? She could feel the question on her lips. Tara knew him. Likely had an inkling what his taste would be. But something held her back—she wasn't completely comfortable with the fact this woman with the dark lipstick and darker hair knew her lover so intimately.

"I'll take it." Imogen reached for her purse.

"Do you want to try it on?"

"No, I'm sure it will be fine."

"Okay, you have seven days to return it with the label on and a receipt anyway."

"That's good."

"Do you want anything else?"

Imogen thought for a moment. The new boots would go with the outfit or the heels she'd brought from home. "No, I think that's all."

Tara rang up the purchase. Two hundred dollars.

Imogen paid and took the bag. "Thank you for your help."

"Any time, and I hope your man, or woman, enjoys the outfit."

"Me too."

Imogen walked past a rack of floggers and paddles and pulled open the door. As it shut behind her, she paused in the recess and tucked her receipt into a side pocket on her bag.

A long, sleek black car drove past. She glanced up—it reminded her of the car Kane used.

It drew to a halt a little way down the street. Where Sub Space was.

She peeked around the corner of the doorway, holding her bag tight. Was the club open in the day?

Two kids on skateboards whizzed past her, then an older woman with a huge white poodle walked quickly by.

The door of the limo opened; the driver got out.

Fuck. She'd seen him before. It *was* Kane's car. Perhaps he let it be used when he was in meetings.

Still half hidden, Imogen watched as the back door was opened. The driver glanced left then right as the passenger stepped out.

Kane.

It was Kane. What the hell was he doing at the club in the middle of the day?

He straightened his tie and said something to the driver. After stepping up to the door, and, like the night before, speaking into the intercom, he was let inside.

Imogen's stomach felt like a lead weight had dropped into it. Kane was at the sex club in the day, without her? What was that all about? Was this his business meeting?

No, that wasn't right.

She pressed her hand over her temple. The driver got back in the car and drove off.

A wave of nausea attacked her and she staggered out onto the pavement, narrowly avoiding bumping into a couple walking hand in hand. "Sorry."

They stared at her and walked on.

*Fuck!*

What should she do? Go to the club and hope last night's password worked? Storm in and demand to know what he was doing?

Of course not. Wouldn't she look stupid then, when she

found him in a meeting about setting up his own clubs in London, Rome, and Berlin.

She quickly went back the way she'd come, heading for Fourth. Going into the club now would be a big mistake. However she found him it wouldn't go well for her.

Because what if she found him with a woman, in a scene?

She swallowed, her throat tight.

Maybe their vanilla sex just hadn't done it for him the night before and he'd had to go and sate his urges. Take a flogger in his hand and beat a lady's ass. Perhaps he didn't feel truly satisfied unless he had kink with his sex and she'd left him wanting.

A tear formed on her lower lid. She'd failed him. Failed the man she wanted to please.

She hurried on, clutching her sexy new outfit. Thoughts of him in there now, wearing his jacket with the stars on, and his mask as he gave another woman pain and pleasure, flashed through her mind.

Eventually, she reached The Four Seasons. She scurried across the lobby, not even saying hello to the concierge, to the suite's private elevator. She jabbed at the button so hard she hurt her finger.

It opened immediately and she stepped in and keyed in the code.

Once alone in the penthouse, she let a sob burst out. She followed it with a sharp huff of frustration.

She had to think rationally and decide what to do—how to handle the situation. She was as good as any of the women in the club; there was no reason she couldn't satisfy Kane Ward. All she had to do was step out of her comfort zone and give it a go—even if it was going to be uncomfortable, in every sense of the word.

# CHAPTER TEN

The hours waiting for Kane to arrive back at the suite dragged. Imogen had tried on her outfit, which fit to perfection. She'd made tea and walked from window to window, staring at New York—which made her wonder even more where he was and what he was doing.

She played the piano, badly, and watched the news. Eventually, she called Clarris.

"Hey, how are you? Have I called too late?" she asked.

"No, it's fine," Clarris answered. "I've just put Katie back to bed; she's had an earache."

"Oh, no."

"She'll be right as rain in the morning, I've dosed her up. How is it going over there?"

"Okay. The private jet was fantastic and the hotel suite is gorgeous. I've been shopping, too, bought some nice bits and pieces including an *I Love New York* t-shirt and teddy for Katie, so cute."

"That's nice."

"And the weather is hot, the sky blue, and—"

"Imogen," Clarris said, her voice stern. "I wasn't really asking about the weather and the hotel. What I meant was what's going on with you and Kane Ward."

"Well, nothing really…" She looked around. That was the truth at this moment in time. And perhaps it had only been a one-night thing…

"Don't give me that. I know you too well. How many bedrooms has this suite got?"

"Er, two."

"And have they both been used?"

"Kind of…"

"Bloody hell, don't be so cagey, I'm not going to write it up in tomorrow's paper. I just want to know how my best friend is getting on with the super-hot, super-rich businessman who's whisked her away to the Big Apple on the pretense that it's all work-related."

"I know, I'm sorry. It's just… complicated."

"How? Tell me."

"Well… we have, he has… you know."

"So you shagged him."

"You could put it like that."

"Good for you, you've had too long a dry spell. Could do with mine ending soon as well." She laughed then the chuckle died away. "Listen, I'm pleased if things are working out for you, really I am, but I've done some digging."

"I don't like the sound of that." Imogen frowned.

Clarris hunted around for information on any new person either of them met.

"Yes, and there's like nothing on him—well, nothing juicy anyway. Hardly any photographs of him other than shaking hands with officials and a few in a karate outfit. Did you know he's a third Dan?"

"What's that?"

"It's karate, he's like a black belt three times over. Takes years to reach that level."

"I know he does karate, he told me that."

"Yes, well, at that level he'd have had to have his hands registered as lethal weapons."

"You're joking?"

Clarris was silent.

She wasn't joking. Imogen thought of Kane's hands on her body the night before, caressing, exploring, bringing her to orgasm. There'd been nothing lethal about them then; dangerous maybe in how expert he was at using them, how he'd got information from her as she'd hovered on the brink of orgasm…

"Imogen. Are you there?"

"Yes. Sorry."

"It's weird, this lack of information. Everyone has something," Clarris went on. "There's not even scorn from a jilted ex or a sniff of scandal in his personal or professional life."

"So, he's been busy building his business, and he's got morals."

"Nah, he's a man who likes money, status, and women. You mark my word, there will be something. No one is as squeaky clean as he is. There's something we don't know, a secret, a past, a crazy wife locked in the attic."

Imogen was quiet. She knew what his dirt was. His penchant for sex clubs and watching and performing in filthy acts. It was clear he'd been very successful at keeping a low profile, at remaining anonymous when indulging his kinky habits.

"Imogen, are you okay?"

"Yes, fine. Listen, I should go, you probably have a million things to be doing if Katie's not well."

"You're right, I have. But call me if you need to."

"I will."

"Promise."

"Promise."

"Miss you, see you when you get back, and have fun breaking that dry spell." She laughed.

"I will, miss you too." Imogen chuckled and hung up. Her smile faded and she sighed.

Clarris certainly had a journalist instinct; she would sniff and sniff. She'd be like a terrier on the trail of a rabbit.

But it wasn't Imogen's place to reveal Kane's secret. She

shuddered; his secret desires splashed around the pages of a newspaper would cause him so much pain. He was such a private man—that much was clear. She didn't want to be part of any kind of public revelation, ever.

She helped herself to several grapes from a large bowl of fruit on the table and thought of the club again. It was a place where Kane clearly felt comfortable and in control. Somewhere he'd wanted to take her. He'd been testing the water about how she felt about his kinky side. Studying her reactions to domination and submission.

There must have been lots of women in his life over the years at clubs like Sub Space. Why hadn't he just chosen one of them to be his lover? Why all the dancing around with her, tricking her into a date at Ascot then whisking her to New York on the pretense—because Clarris had been right, that's what it was—of it being a business trip?

She walked across an Oriental carpet, the threads soft on her bare feet. Was it because he just fancied her? Old-fashioned boy meets girl and wants girl to be his?

But it wasn't that simple, was it? He wanted her to be his, but to conform to his sexual appetites and sample the flavors he enjoyed. He'd said last night was vanilla, and for her it was perfect, but clearly he wanted to taste more and he couldn't do that alone.

She slid her hands over her backside. He wanted to flog her, spank her, tie her up. There was no way she could deny the thought thrilled her as much as it made her belly tense with apprehension.

And if she did submit, would that mean he wouldn't go to the clubs anymore? If they started a kinky relationship, would he be hers and hers alone?

That thought appealed to her very much. Kane Ward had been on her radar for a long time, and now that things were happening between them, she didn't want to mess it up. She admired him, fancied him, loved spending time with him. Which meant it was worth a go. She had to step into his world and be fully committed to trying on his kink and giving it a shot.

"Yes." She clapped. "No more questions, just do it." She glanced at a clock above the fireplace. It was nearly four. "No time like the present."

She hurried into the bedroom and pulled out the pretty basque she'd bought earlier in the day. Quickly, she stripped out of her jeans and t-shirt and put it on. She removed her knickers then slipped into the stockings and her high heels.

She paused at the mirror on her way out of the room. "Bloody hell." She looked sexy and flushed. The basque was beautiful, her pussy hair the same dark shade as the material.

She spotted the collar on the dressing table and reached for it. She secured it around her neck, knowing he liked her to wear it.

After a hastily applied slick of bright red lipstick, she walked into the main room.

From the hallway she heard a ping. The elevator had been called down to reception. He was here.

She rushed to the piano and stretched herself over it, ass in the air. The wooden surface was cool against her skin as she rested her cheek on it and stared out at the rooftops.

God, what was she doing?

What if it wasn't him?

What if he had company?

She lifted up. Glanced over at the bedroom door. Should she dart back inside?

Fuck it. This was her plan. She could do this.

She tipped forward again, parted her legs. When he walked from the hall area into the main room, he'd see her buttocks facing him and waiting to be reddened. He'd see her pussy peeking out, ready to be fucked.

She swallowed; her mouth was dry and her heart tripping along. As she breathed, the warm air from her lungs fogged the surface of the piano.

A distant swoosh signaled that the elevator had arrived.

She strained to listen. Hoping to hell she wouldn't hear voices.

She didn't.

After a few seconds, the elevator doors shut and one set of footsteps walked into the room.

She stayed utterly still.

He stopped.

She clenched her fists.

"Imogen," he said, a question sitting in the way he'd spoken.

"I want you to spank me, flog me, do whatever it is you need to do." She moved her hips from left to right.

"That's a very tempting offer."

She glanced over her shoulder and saw him shrug out of his suit jacket. He draped it over the sofa and took a step closer.

"I'm sorry if I didn't hit the spot for you last night," she said. "Do whatever you need to do to me now."

"Why would you say that about last night?"

He walked right up to the piano, but instead of stopping behind her, as she'd expected him to, he sat at the stool in front of the keys and looked up at her.

"Because I know what you're into and we didn't do that. None of it."

"I told you sometimes vanilla is the best flavor."

"But—"

"I've wanted you for a long time, Imogen. I needed nothing more than to make love to you the way I did last night." He smiled and closed the case over the keys. "There was nothing lacking, nothing at all, so please don't think that was the case." He paused. "Unless there was something missing for you?"

"No, no, there wasn't." She shut her eyes. Damn it. She'd been stupid to offer her bare ass to him. He'd think she was mad or certainly naïve.

"I'm glad to hear it," he said. He raised his right hand and undid the cuff. He then rolled it three times, very neatly, very precisely.

Imogen watched as he repeated the action with his left

sleeve. When he'd done it, she started to stand straight.

"No," he said, setting his gaze on her. "Stay like that."

The tremble in her belly intensified, and she draped herself back over the piano.

"You just invited me to spank your pretty ass," he said.

"Yes."

"Does the invitation still stand?"

"Yes."

*God, this is it.*

A slow smile spread on his face. "The thing is, though, my beautiful Imogen, you're not quite ready for it." He stood and walked to her side, placed his hand at the small of her back.

"I'm not?"

"No. You still have something to learn before my handprints adorn your buttocks." He smoothed his hand over her ass cheeks, each one in turn. "And fine buttocks they are. I can hardly wait but I will resist."

Imogen bit her bottom lip. Was he resisting because he'd already had his pleasure for the day?

"Kane…?" she asked.

"Yes?" He slipped his hand between her legs and dipped into her dampness.

"You went to the club, today."

He stilled. "Yes. How—?"

"I saw you. I was shopping nearby."

He stroked over her ass again, soft sweeping movements. "Quite a coincidence in a city of millions."

She was quiet. There was no need to justify it—it had been a coincidence.

"I had a meeting with my friend," he said. "Who owns the club. There was something I wanted from him and he's agreed. It was one of those requests that needed to be made in person."

"Okay." Relief swept through her. So he hadn't been in a scene, making love, fucking someone else as she'd paced the floor.

"It will all become clear," he said. "You must trust me."

"I do."

"Do you?" He pulled gently but firmly at her upper arm, forcing her to stand straight. "Do you really?"

"Yes." She looked into his eyes. "Yes, I do."

"I'm not just talking about trusting me in the everyday sense of the word. This is much more, much deeper."

"Tell me, Kane. Don't talk in riddles."

He shook his head and turned away. "Fuck, this is happening much faster than I planned."

"What is?"

"This. I wanted it to be normal between us..." He looked back at her, his gaze sweeping over the basque.

"Really? How can you say that when you took me to Sub Space last night?"

"I just wanted you to get a taste of it. I didn't expect this... coming back to the offer of spanking your ass. You're not ready."

"You said that before, but don't I get a say in it?"

"If I really was your master, no, you wouldn't." He touched the collar about her neck and ran his finger around it, just brushing her skin.

"Kane," she said quietly. "Don't open a door for me then tell me not to step through it."

He swallowed and his Adam's apple bobbed beneath his shirt. "I just don't want to scare you away. I'm..." He pressed his lips together and shook his head slightly.

"Intense, hot, different."

"Yes, different, certainly compared to any other man you've been with."

"How do you know?"

He gave a half shrug. "I know."

She couldn't argue the case. He was right. He was different in so many ways. "I do trust you."

"With your body? With your pleasure, with your pain, with everything I can give you and the new places I can take you to?"

"Yes. You're an expert at what you do, isn't that what the stars mean on your jacket?" She reached out and pressed over his shirt where she knew his three tattoos were. "And what you have here?"

He placed his hand over hers. "Yes, that is what the stars mean."

"So show me. I couldn't be in any safer or more qualified hands, could I?"

He shook his head. She wasn't sure if it meant he wouldn't show her or if he really thought he was the best man for the job.

"Kane?"

"You're right, I shouldn't have whet your appetite then told you off for wanting to take a bite. I should have guessed that's how this would go. You're inquisitive, intelligent, brave; it's those qualities that I admire about you."

*He did?* "So you'll show me?"

"Yes. But we're starting at the basics."

"That works for me." A flutter of triumph swept through her.

"A foundation for us to build on." He stepped back and stared at the window.

Imogen let her arms hang at her sides. What would he want her to do? She had no idea what he meant by the basics.

He set his attention on her again and reached for his belt buckle.

*Oh, fuck.* He was going to strike her with the belt. She'd wondered if that was his thing last night, when he'd taken it off and wound it around his hand. It was the way his muscles had tensed, how he'd held it, the electricity that had seared through the air, almost sizzling from him.

The belt would hurt like hell. She'd imagined his hand or a paddle, the flogger something to work toward. But the belt...

He undid the buckle, then again slid it slowly from the loops. Once it was free, he let the belt hang down, the end skimming the floor. "Go and kneel in the center of that rug."

She did as he'd asked, aware of her heels pressing on her bare buttocks as she got to her knees.

He moved behind her. "Wrists together."

She pressed her hands close and linked her fingers.

He wound the belt around her forearms—not tight, loose, very loose, so much so that she could easily have shaken it away. If she'd moved her arms it would have fallen.

"Now keep still," he said. "Imagine you're bound tight, by rope. It's thick and rough and you're trapped by it."

"Yes."

"Sir." He cupped her chin and raised her face to his. "Yes, *Sir.*"

"Yes, Sir," she said.

A light had come on in his eyes; excitement, maybe? That he was being the person he was comfortable with? Having her kneeling before him? Or was it a combination of all three?

"I'm always *Sir* when you're submitting to me. Which is what you're doing now."

She continued to gaze up at him.

"Cast your gaze down, at the floor." He pressed the top of her head. "A good sub only looks at her master if given permission, and not only that, a good sub only speaks when her master gives her permission."

Imogen stared at an intricate pattern on the rug.

"You may speak."

"Yes, Sir."

"Do you know what else a good sub does?"

"No, Sir."

"A good sub always remembers their safe word."

"I don't have one… Sir."

"So think of one. Nothing else can happen until you have told me what it is."

She was quiet, her brain spinning. What should she

choose?

"I'll pick for you," he said after several seconds. "Westminster Abbey."

"Yes, Sir."

"Repeat it."

"Westminster Abbey."

"If I do or say anything that goes beyond what you can cope with, what's pleasurable, all you have to do is say Westminster Abbey and it all ends."

"Okay."

"Never forget it."

"I won't."

"It is of upmost importance that Westminster Abbey remains in your mind, even when you feel high, floaty, spinning, you must remember that's your safe word, your safe place. Can you picture it?"

"Yes." She shut her eyes and pictured the Abbey before her—she'd visited it several times. "It's beautiful."

"Just like you." He stroked his hand down her cheek to her chin then up to her opposite temple. "Your skin is like silk," he said. "The finest silk."

She didn't answer.

He trailed his hand down to her shoulder. "And the color of porcelain."

He was almost speaking to himself.

"I've thought of this," he said, "many times. Of showing you what your body can do when it truly connects with your mind." He cupped her right breast over the basque. "The mind is so powerful. Giving yourself over, mind and body, to another person can be incredibly freeing. That's what makes the binds all the sweeter—they'll free you as much as they restrain you. Though not today, my darling, today you can move your arms at will, but I hope you'll consent to being bound by me one day."

"Yes, Sir."

He hooked his thumb beneath her chin and raised her face again. "Look at me."

She did. Right into his beautiful eyes.

He stooped, bent lower and lower still, then pressed his mouth over hers. He kissed her deeply, softly, his tongue probing.

Imogen found herself straining for more. The belt around her arms shifted. She wished it were tighter, that he had harnessed her firmly.

"And you taste," he said, pulling back, "like the sweetest fruit, like everything I've ever wanted." He frowned, stood tall, and pushed his hand through his hair.

Imogen watched him. He seemed to be composing himself.

*What the hell does he really want to do?*

He turned and walked to the opposite end of the rug. He breathed deep, several times, his ribs expanding beneath his shirt.

She was about to speak but clamped her mouth. She wasn't to talk without permission. It was a strange concept, but surprisingly it came naturally.

He looked at her again. Flexed his fingers, then balled them into fists.

Imogen dropped her gaze to the floor.

Within seconds she was staring at his polished shoes.

"Submitting," he said. "is about obeying. Do you understand?"

"Yes, Sir."

# CHAPTER ELEVEN

"Are you willing to obey?" Kane asked.

"Yes, Sir," Imogen replied.

"Then that will be today's lesson." He ran his hand into her hair and collected it in a bunch. He fisted it, forcing her to look up at him. "Do you have any questions?"

Imogen could feel the basque moving against her body with her rapid breaths. An image flashed through her mind: Tara, at the club, obeying her master, being strung up and flogged, then coming. Her master had done that, taken her there. But what about him? He hadn't climaxed.

"Yes," she said. "One."

"Then ask." He frowned slightly.

"At the club, the second scene. Tara's master didn't come—how does that work? How is that good for him?"

"Excellent question." With his free hand, he popped open the top button on his suit trousers. "When two or three or more people are in a scene it's not a requirement for everyone to come together. Vanilla couples put too much emphasis on that—what is it, the holy bloody grail to climax in unison?" He drew down the zipper on his fly. "In this world you're stepping into, giving pleasure is as wonderful as receiving pleasure."

She stared at his groin. His cock was straining behind the material.

"There will be times a master gives his sub pleasure and he goes without, yet feels fully satisfied, and times when a sub gives pleasure without receiving." He shoved at his trousers and they slipped down his thighs, exposing his hairy legs. He then tugged at the waistband of his boxer briefs and pushed them out of the way.

His cock sprang forward, long and thick and twisted with veins. The head was shiny and domed, and the shaft emerged from a tangle of dark hair.

Imogen stared at it. In the harsh light of day it was beet red, the veins bruised blue.

He took it in his fist and rubbed up then down the length of it. "A master owns his sub's body." He paused. "In this moment, right now, do I own yours?"

She clenched her pussy muscles. "Yes, Sir."

"Good." He stepped closer. He held her face, beneath her chin, and his fingers and thumb rested on her cheeks. "Open up."

She stared at him and did as he'd asked. She opened her mouth, knowing what was about to happen. She could hardly wait to taste him. Excitement raced through her nerves.

"Wider," he said, pressing on the hollows in her cheeks.

She did as he'd instructed, opening so wide her jaw ached.

He slipped the head of his cock over her lips. "Jesus, it's so hot to see you like this." There was awe in his tone. "I'm going to fuck your mouth now, Imogen. Can you handle that?"

She gave a half nod.

He slid in another inch, spreading his flavor—man and musk and a hint of salt.

She wrapped her tongue around his girth, holding him with it.

He released his cock and took hold of her hair again,

gripping it tight. He moaned and pushed in another inch.

"That's it," he said. "Take my cock in your mouth so deep, so deep I'm part of you."

She strained toward him, eager for more. Giving oral sex hadn't been one of her favorite pastimes with previous partners, but damn, with Kane, she wanted more, she wanted all of it.

He withdrew, then pushed back in. Saliva coated his cock and dripped onto her chin.

She tipped forward, then leaned back.

"Keep still." His grip tightened in her hair and he held her steady. He pumped his hips, fucking her mouth as though it was her pussy. A low groan rumbled up from his chest.

She tasted a drip of pre-cum and went to move her arms, wanting to grab his ass, cup his balls, touch him. But the belt reminded her that she was tied—psychologically if not physically. She stilled.

Sweat collected in her cleavage and her pussy was damp with arousal.

"Yes, yes, like that, with your tongue," he said, his voice ragged. "Keep going... Jesus Christ..."

She continued with the soft dragging suction she'd created on the base of his shaft.

"Oh, fuck, you're going to have to swallow, sub," he said, then gasped.

He was coming—she could feel it. She was so excited stars danced behind her closed eyelids. Her pussy clenched and her clit was swollen.

A shot of cum hit the back of her throat. She swallowed it as he continued to thrust in and out of her mouth. She felt used but also adored. It was her—her body that made him feel this way.

He groaned and his cock pulsed in her mouth. "Keep... taking me," he said, pulling completely out, then smoothing back in so deep her nose nestled in his pubic hair. "All of me."

She did, taking him until his balls nudged up against her chin and he filled her throat. She wasn't sure, but a small tremble, not unlike an orgasm, glided over her skin. She was his, completely his in that moment. She hoped he thought of nothing else but her. Her mouth, her tongue, her throat. Surely making his millions was the furthest thing from his mind right now.

"Thank you," he said, pulling out and once again tipping her head to look at him. "You pleased me very well."

She pulled in a couple of quick breaths. Her lips felt stretched and tight at the corners. Her chin was wet. "I'm glad."

He smiled. "Sir."

"I'm glad, Sir." Her heart swelled—it wasn't love, was it? But there was something big building between them. A connection of souls, attraction so deep it didn't need words.

He reached for his clothing. Tucked his dick away and snapped up the zipper on his trousers. After stepping behind her, he untangled the belt from her arms.

"How do you feel?" he asked, walking in front of her and slotting his belt back into place.

Imogen studied the floor again and thought for a moment. "I feel... like my mind is clear. Not as much now the belt has gone, but everything faded away when you were in control."

"I'm still in control." He sat on the sofa opposite her.

"Yes, Sir." She looked at him.

"Yes, you may raise your head," he said, stretching his arm over the back of the seat and smiling, just a little. He crossed his right ankle over his left knee. "And what are you thinking?"

"That I feel satisfied. Like I did last night."

"Good, if you feel like that, then your first lesson has been a success." He paused. "But I always knew you'd be a good student."

"Student?"

"I hoped you'd be this keen to learn. Let's just say

118

nothing about you, Imogen, has ever disappointed me and I hope it stays that way."

She had a sudden feeling that he might not just be talking about sex and kink, that there were undercurrents to his words. Kane had become a man she wanted to please in every aspect of his life. She couldn't deny it any longer; she was falling fast, faster than a rock in a puddle.

"So, food," he said. "Shall we get room service?"

"Whatever pleases you, Sir."

He smiled. "You can go and get dressed, Imogen. I'll organize something for us to eat."

Imogen stood—her knees were stiff.

"Are you okay?" he asked, leaning forward as if about to stand.

"I'm fine, really." She held up her hand. "I'll be back in a minute."

She walked toward the bedroom, acutely aware of her naked backside. She felt almost like she was gliding. What they'd just done... it was so erotic, so utterly different to anything else she'd ever experienced in her sex life. It stoked a fire and created a hunger in her. Kane Ward had opened her mind and her body to a new way to be, and there was no going back now.

He'd changed her forever.

• • • • • • •

Imogen removed the basque and pulled on underwear, jeans, and a white t-shirt. She splashed water on her face and brushed her hair. A feeling of calm settled over her. She hadn't been spanked, as she'd been prepared to be, but Kane had taken her to a new high. She couldn't imagine anyone but him taking her there. She wouldn't drop to her knees and open her mouth for any other man. As for swallowing, she'd enjoyed that too, had loved every bit of it.

He was special, she knew that, and he was also worming his way into her heart.

When she wandered, barefoot, back into the living area, Kane was on the telephone, staring out of the window by the piano.

"Yes, I understand," he said. "Completely, which is why I want you to do exactly as instructed."

Imogen poured a glass of water from a pitcher that had slices of lemon floating in it.

"The CEO will give us what we want," Kane went on. "He just needs a little more pressure, then he'll cave. It's the best thing for his company at the end of the day. Without us propping up the assets while he rides this storm, it's the end of Global Tech Limited and he loves that company." He paused. "Damon, I get that you're concerned, but I'm not. Do as we discussed."

Imogen sipped her water and studied his broad shoulders and the way his white shirt had stretched between them. He stood with his feet hip-width apart, and she took a moment to enjoy the view of his ass. It had been so good to grip it the night before. She hoped she'd get the chance to again soon.

"Okay," Kane said, "so that's settled. I'll expect you to call by tomorrow afternoon with the deal in the bag. Take him for dinner tonight as planned, put the squeeze on, let him know he can trust us after he's signed on the dotted line." He was quiet for a moment. "Perfect, great choice. Yes, I'll speak to you tomorrow, go do what you're good at." He clicked his phone shut and turned.

"Problems?" Imogen asked, sitting on the chair and folding her legs beneath her.

"No, not at all." He smiled. "I have one more call to make, is that all right with you?"

"Of course."

He pressed a couple of buttons on his phone, then held it to his ear. "How are you?" He'd grinned as he'd spoken. "Yes. I'm in New York, you know I am, but obviously not at my place." He laughed at the reply. "Four Seasons, but it's not too shabby."

His voice held a different tone to the last call; he was more relaxed and pleased to be talking to whoever was on the other end of the line. This wasn't work.

"How about tomorrow evening?" He glanced at Imogen. "And I've got someone I'd like you to meet." He listened to a long reply.

Imogen smiled. It must be his brother he was talking to.

"Well, seems like it will be a table for four then," Kane said. "I'll have my PA book us something and she'll let you know." He laughed. "Yeah, see you then." He placed his phone on the side.

"Who was that?" Imogen asked, resting back on the cushions.

"That," Kane said, placing his hands on the arms of her chair and leaning over so their faces were close, "was my brother, Taylor. We're going out for dinner with him and his new lady tomorrow night."

"You really want to introduce me to your family already?" She raised her eyebrows and gave him a cheeky smile.

"I told you," he said, kissing her. "I've waited too long for all of this and I'm not a man who likes to wait; if I'm honest, it's tested my patience." He touched his lips to hers. "Now that it's finally happening, I'm struggling to not let it just explode." He paused. "Besides, it feels so right, doesn't it?"

She touched his cheek. "Yes, it does."

A softness spread over his features. "I'm glad you feel that way too."

"I've waited for this as well, Kane. There's been a spark between us since the first time we met."

"Yes, it was ignited by that tight red skirt you wore that showed a fraction more thigh than is proper for a bank manager. It had me hard enough to hammer nails in that first meeting."

She gasped. "It was not... you were not."

He laughed. "Why would I lie?"

"Because…" She giggled. "I like that skirt."

"So do I."

"I can't wear it for work now that you've said that."

"No, I don't think you can. But that will suit me to know it's for my eyes only."

She smoothed her hand down his neck and rested her fingers on the collar of his shirt. How would this work out in the future for them? Kane spoke like there was more, like they'd be an item, but he was rarely in London. His meetings at the bank were months apart; he spent most of his time jetting around the globe. Yet her job was very much office-based—central London office-based.

"What's up?" he asked, a slight frown marring his brow.

"Nothing, nothing at all." She smiled. "Did you organize food?"

"Yes, sushi, is that okay?"

"Mmm… perfect." It was one of her favorite things to eat.

•••••••

They sat at a mahogany table overlooking Central Park and dined on delicious smoked salmon nigiri, prawn temaki, and tuna sashimi. The suite's private butler had placed a bottle of pale white wine in an ice bucket, and when he'd left them alone, Kane poured them both a glass.

"This is wonderful," Imogen said, gesturing at the food, then the view. "Perfect."

"I'm glad you think so." He expertly captured a stray grain of rice in his chopsticks. "You like to travel. Where else have you been?"

"I've seen a bit of the US with work, skied in the Alps and spent some time in Spain with my friend, Clarris. Other than Thailand this year, that's it." She helped herself to another sliver of salmon.

"I'd like to show you more of the world."

"I'd like that." She smiled at him. "Clarris went to Japan

with work last year; she said I'd love it."

"What does she do, Clarris?"

"She's a journalist."

He nodded slowly. "Do you see her often?"

"Yes, she lives next door. She has a little one, Katie; she's adorable."

"Pretty name."

"She's a pretty girl."

Kane was quiet.

Imogen wasn't sure if he was thinking about Clarris' work as a journalist and wondering if that could have implications for him, or if he was thinking about Katie, about having children of his own.

"Do you want a family one day?" she asked.

He jerked his head a little, as though surprised by her question. He quickly composed himself. "Do you?"

"Yes. I think so. But not the way Clarris did it. She fell pregnant on a one-night stand with a married man. She's on her own one hundred percent. Well, she's got me, but it's not the same."

"That's hard."

"Yes. She told the father, but he wanted nothing to do with either her or the baby. He said that his wife was also pregnant and she was his priority and they were going to make a go of it."

"Bastard."

"Yes, we called him that, and more." Imogen shrugged. It had been a very difficult time for Clarris. "But you didn't answer my question."

"No."

"No, you didn't answer my question, or no, you don't want kids?"

He looked out at the skyline. "I do want children. I'd love to have a son or daughter to pass everything on to; it would make all of this, my achievements feel more solid, worthwhile, I suppose... but..."

"But what?"

"But I feel…" He rubbed his eyebrow with the tip of his finger. "I only ever do anything if I'm sure I can do it perfectly, and having kids and trying to stay on top of the business, could I do both?"

"I suppose that's a question every parent asks themselves. Both are full-time jobs." She took a sip of wine. "Which is why some people say two parents are better than one, it doubles the available time."

He looked back at her. "I'm away a lot. I'm barely in London."

"I know."

"I'd hardly even know where to base a family." He shook his head. "It took me so long to be able to schedule this, us."

"Schedule?"

"Yes, I could hardly seduce you on a conference call." He laughed. "It took quite a bit of planning to get you here, with me."

"I don't think I was that hard to catch." She thought of how he'd tricked her into going to the races.

"I'm not sure if I've caught you yet." He reached for his drink, took a sip, and studied her over the rim of his glass.

*You have.* "Anyway, I didn't mean that I wanted to have your babies next week," she said, then laughed to lighten the mood. "I was just curious as to what you saw in your future."

"Curious is good." He set down his drink and glanced at his watch. "Which brings us to the next part of our evening."

She raised her eyebrows. "That sounds interesting."

"We're going back to the club."

"What, now?"

"Yes. It's all arranged. Did you get something else to wear or are you planning on the same dress as last night?"

Imogen's heart rate picked up. She hadn't expected to be slipping into her sexy all-in-one outfit so soon. "Yes, I got something."

He smiled—one of his smiles that went right to his eyes and sent creases shooting out from the corners. "Good. We'll leave in one hour."

# CHAPTER TWELVE

Kane pressed the buzzer on the door and spoke into the small meshed speaker. "Red Queen."

Imogen pulled the long beige coat around herself and glanced left then right. It wasn't yet dark and being on the streets of New York in her super-sexy outfit made her self-conscious.

The door opened. Aisha stood in the small hallway in yet another skintight PVC dress, this time bright green. "Master K," she said. "What a treat to see you twice in as many days."

Kane took Imogen's hand and stepped in. "Thank you, Aisha."

She held out a long chrome key. "I have instructions to leave you alone."

"There is no one else here?" Kane asked, taking the key.

"No. The club is completely empty. I'm the last one. If you lock this door only you can let anyone else in."

"Good, that is what I'd arranged with Master Dean."

Aisha smiled. "I hope you enjoy your time here." She glanced at Imogen—there was more warmth in her smile than there had been the day before. "And your sub experiences what you want her to."

"Thank you," Kane said. "I'm sure she will."

Kane slotted the key in the lock, his action signaling it was time for Aisha to leave.

She took the hint and, pulling a small black purse over her shoulder, headed out.

Kane shut the door and turned the key.

The click of metal sliding into place rattled around Imogen's head. Kane had arranged to have the entire club emptied, just for them? Excitement spun through her mind as nerves fluttered in her stomach.

"Now," he said, reaching for the belt of her coat. "You can be really honest about what you see here, tell me everything that goes through your mind, what interests you, what excites you." He released the knot and pushed the material from her shoulders. "I want to know what you'd like to try and what you think your limits would be." He hung her coat on a hook, then added his light jacket next to it.

He was wearing a black shirt and neat black jeans that accentuated his height, slim hips, and wide shoulders.

"How long? I mean when...?"

"We can stay as long as we want to. Sub Space won't be open tonight." He surveyed her body, seeing her outfit properly for the first time.

"Because of us?"

"Yes, because of us. I didn't think you'd want an audience, not yet anyway."

Her mouth was a little dry. She swallowed.

"Don't be so worried. You want this, you told me so, you're curious."

"Yes, I am." She tilted her chin. "And I'm not worried." She nodded at the door to the room they'd went into the day before. "Are you going to put your velvet jacket on?"

"No. I'm your master; you don't need to see the stars on the jacket to remember that."

"You have them on your body."

"Exactly." He reached for her hand and led her down

the narrow corridor they'd used yesterday to get to the bar area.

Once more, Imogen stared at the women in the pictures bound by rope. There appeared to be real art to the knots and symmetry in the design.

"Beautiful, aren't they?" Kane said.

"Yes, very."

"It's called shibari, an art form that can take years to perfect."

"Can you do it?"

"Of course."

"Oh, okay."

"Would you like me to tie you like that?" He gestured to the picture next to them.

It was of a woman with black poker-straight hair. She was bound over her chest so that her breasts bulged forward, swollen and bloated. The rope went around her waist, between her legs and down to her ankles. Her arms were behind her back—Imogen guessed they were also secured—and she stared at the camera with a defiant expression.

"I don't know." That was the honest answer. "Wouldn't it take a long time to do and then undo?"

"Yes, but what's the rush? If she's enjoying her master's attention and he's enjoying the art of shibari, then it works for both."

"And when she's like that? Tied up. Then what?"

"Well, then he can do whatever he wants to her."

Imogen looked at the photograph again. She couldn't imagine being tied like that. Which didn't mean she wouldn't try it; she just couldn't picture herself in that position.

"You'd be so beautiful in rope," Kane said, touching his lips to her cheek. "Perhaps one day... soon I'll get to see your pale skin bound by my ropes and your breasts squeezed like that."

"Perhaps." She shifted. Her outfit was so tight it was

almost like being bound now. She liked it, though, it was sexy, and knowing the zips could be undone and her body exposed added to the thrill.

"Come on," Kane said, "this way."

He led her into the drinks area. It was quiet and still, the bar shiny and clear of glasses. The cushions on the chairs were all neat and straight and several candles, in small jars, sent flickers up the walls and over the ceiling.

"Give me a twirl," he said, holding her at arm's length. "Let me get a proper look at this. You were secretive back in the apartment, putting that coat straight over the top."

She smiled and did as he'd asked, rolling her hips as she walked in a circle, her high heels clicking on the hard floor.

"That's definitely not one for the office," he said. He stepped closer. "It would be better like this, though." He reached for the zipper that circled around her right breast. He undid it, slowly, the material peeling away from the rest of the outfit. Once it was detached, he dropped it on a nearby table and studied Imogen's naked breast protruding from the gap.

Her nipple was tight and erect.

He reached for the other zipper and repeated his actions.

Now she had both breasts exposed. He'd been right to hire the place exclusively—she wouldn't have been comfortable like this, especially without the mask.

"It's stunning," he said, skimming his hands down her waist and over her hips. "*You're* stunning." He pursed his lips and blew out a breath. "I'm so happy you're here."

"I'm happy to be here." She adored seeing desire in his eyes; it was rich and reflected her own longing.

He took both her nipples and rolled them between his fingers and thumbs. "We have to make the most of our time."

"Yes," she managed.

"Every moment with you is precious."

She felt the same. What they had was special—scary exciting sexy special.

He released her nipples and reached into the pocket of his trousers. "Will you wear this again?" He withdrew the collar.

"If you want me to."

"Yes, very much so. It completes the look." He paused. "Plus, it means you've submitted to me, your master, and I have control. When you wear this, you're mine."

Imogen didn't think Kane needed collars to have control over her, or anyone else, but she'd wear it because he wanted her to. Also, it did feel nice around her neck; the symbolism of it warmed her. She liked being his... a lot.

She held up her hair and turned.

Gently, he slipped it on, then checked that it wasn't too tight by sliding a finger between the leather and her throat. "So damn sexy," he murmured against her ear. "Come on, let's go through to the playroom."

She released her hair and it swished down her back. She then allowed him to lead her through the metal mesh curtain into the room they'd watched the scenes in the night before.

Again the lights were dim, but each cubicle was lit, highlighting the bench, the cross, a table with stirrups, and a cage. It seemed strange without an audience, as if the equipment was sleeping somehow.

She could still smell sex, even though the large room was empty. Arousal and lust seemed to linger in the air, giving it a rich, musky scent.

Kane left her side and walked to the first cubicle. In it was a large black wheel with about a two-meter diameter. He spun it. "Do you fancy this?" he asked. "Being attached, ankles and wrists, and spun?"

"Er, I'm not sure that I do. I get seasick..." It didn't appeal to Imogen. Where was the fun in being spun like a fairground ride?

"It is very popular with some submissives." He frowned a little.

"I'm sure. But not me." She folded her arms, but changed her mind when she remembered her naked breasts.

"I think you're forgetting something." He frowned.

"What?"

"What, *Sir*." His frown deepened.

"Sorry, Sir." But she still didn't fancy the wheel.

"Remember to address me correctly when you're wearing the collar," he said, moving to the next cubicle.

Imogen walked with him.

"How about this?" He lifted the lid on a wire cage. "Would you like it in here? Bound and waiting for me?"

"No, I bloody wouldn't!" Was he mad? How was a cage sexy?

"I won't tell you again." He dropped the lid with a crash.

"What?"

"What, *Sir*!" His voice was loud and echoed around the cubicle.

"I'm sorry, *Sir*. But it will always be no because how is a cage fun?"

"For some it is an expression of their total obedience and trust in their master." He tilted his chin and studied her. "That is what you need to understand."

Imogen held his gaze. She was curious about spanking and submission and even bondage and anal sex, but going in a cage like an animal—it wasn't for her.

"Touch that collar about your neck," he said.

She did as he'd asked.

"Remember what it means, remember what I told you earlier. When you're wearing that, I am Sir and you only look at me when given permission."

She held his stare for a moment, unable to hide defiance, then dropped her gaze to the floor. "Yes... Sir," she mumbled.

He walked up to her, his footsteps heavy on the floor.

He came close, so close she could feel his body heat on her naked breasts.

"Be careful," he said.

Imogen bit on her bottom lip. She didn't trust herself to speak.

He stepped away.

She watched him move into another cubicle. This one contained what appeared to be a board that a person could be strapped onto.

Kane released a lever and pushed the top of the board. The whole thing tipped, completely, so that if anyone had been on it they'd be upside down.

"What the…?" she murmured, wondering how a head rush could be erotic.

"This," Kane said, "is very popular and you shouldn't rule it out until you've tried it."

"Jesus, you want me to have a headache all night? That's hardly going to be conducive to sexy times." As she'd spoken she knew full well she'd been out of line. Not only had she not tagged Sir onto the end, she'd stared right at him.

He pressed his lips together and his chest expanded. In ten big strides he was beside her.

Suddenly, Imogen found herself in exactly the position she'd just scorned—inverted.

He'd tipped her over his knee as he'd sat hastily on the nearest sofa.

"Hey," she gasped, the world turning upside down and her hair falling over her face and sweeping onto the floor. "What…?"

"I gave you plenty of warning," he said, clamping her legs between his and pressing between her shoulder blades.

A hard whack landed on her ass, then another and another.

"What the…? Ow…" She squirmed and tried to protect her ass with her hands.

He pushed them away and continued to rain slaps over her leather-clad buttocks.

It hurt. It hurt like hell. The sharp sting of each connection raced over her skin, the material seeming to smart against her.

"Get off," she said, pushing at the floor. It was no good,

she was well and truly trapped by his powerful thighs.

"This is what… happens when subs… disrespect their masters," he said, the words huffing out between slaps.

"Kane!" She tried to twist to no avail. Her ass was on fire. "It hurts, fuck…" And the humiliation of being upended like a naughty toddler, Jesus. She screwed up her eyes and again pushed at the floor.

"Keep still," he said.

"Kane, stop it… ow."

Tears began to swell behind her closed lids. This wasn't fun, it hurt. It wasn't what she'd expected. There was nothing sensual about it. She was hot, dizzy, her tight outfit was suffocating her. "Kane!"

He increased the speed of the slaps, the sound ringing through her ears the way it was scorching over her buttocks. Breathing was getting difficult; a sob burst upward and came out as a yelp.

"Get off…" she gasped again, wincing at an extra hard slap. "Fuck! Get off." She clenched her fists. "Westminster Abbey… Westminster fucking Abbey, all right? Get off."

The slapping stopped. Between one heartbeat and the next she was righted and half-sat, half-laid onto the sofa.

"Fuck," he said. His cheeks were flushed. He was staring straight at her.

"What the hell was that…?" Imogen snapped, shuffling backward until her shoulders hit the arm of the seat.

"I'm sorry," he said, shoving his hand through his hair and shaking his head.

"Yeah, well… at least now I know the safe word works."

"It will always work." He moved closer, crawled up the sofa, then spread himself over her. "I'm sorry to have made you have to use it."

Imogen looked at his face. There was anxiety there, and sorrow. She hated seeing sadness in his eyes. "What the hell was that all about, though?" Her buttocks were tingling like crazy; it was though a swarm of bees had stung them.

"You disobeyed me," he said softly.

"No, I didn't."

"I wanted to know which piece of equipment you were keen to try and you were dismissive of everything I showed you." He pushed a lock of hair that had become stuck to her damp cheek. "*And* you kept forgetting to call me Sir."

"So that's what I get? Tipped over and spanked like a toddler?"

"Not like a child, Imogen, like a submissive who has stepped out of line."

"But I thought the spanking was for fun, when playing in a scene."

"What do you think the D stands for in BDSM?"

"I don't know, and I don't know all the rules either. You need to remember that."

"I'm teaching you the rules." He paused. "D stands for Discipline, Imogen. When you're wearing my collar and you don't behave, it is my responsibility to discipline you. I am your dominant, another word that starts with D incidentally, and it is up to me to keep you in line."

"But I'm a grown woman, I don't need you to spank me for misbehaving. And I don't think you should get to decide if I have misbehaved."

"Are you sure?"

"Yes. We're both adults." Imogen shut her eyes. Maybe this wasn't for her after all. Perhaps she'd been wrong to think she could try on Kane's kink and it would fit.

"What are you thinking?" he asked, his chest touching her naked breasts.

"I'm thinking that's not for me, the spanking for being… naughty. I hold down an important job, make big decisions, it's too… humiliating."

"So you didn't like it one bit?"

"Not like that, no. I didn't. The reason for it was all wrong in my mind."

He studied her. His cock was erect and nudged at her thigh. "I'm sorry. I pushed too far."

"You just did what you do here, in your world. But it's

not mine."

He glanced away.

A nugget of fear landed in Imogen's mind. Was this it? They weren't compatible. Would he tell her it was time to leave and whatever was growing between them would be crushed?

"Kane," she pressed her palm to his cheek, "give me a chance, this is all moving so fast. This time last week I wouldn't have entertained wearing an outfit like this, or coming to a place where live sex was the entertainment, but I'm here. I'm giving it a go. I'm trying."

He looked back down at her. "And I'm glad you are. Really glad."

She smiled gently. "And I certainly wouldn't have... earlier..."

"What? You wouldn't have what earlier?"

She hesitated then, "Swallowed your cum."

He raised his eyebrows. "I'm honored."

"So you should be." She giggled and a flush rose up her neck to her face.

He kissed her hot cheek. "You're blushing."

"I know. It's not under my control."

"Now you know how I feel... with you."

"Maybe I'm not a very good submissive."

He dropped his weight over her a little more, settling his legs between hers. "I think you're a fine submissive. This is all my fault and I feel ashamed to be a dom of my status to have got it so wrong."

"Kane, I—"

"I took it too fast, I was greedy."

"But you stopped when I needed you to."

"Are you sure you're okay?"

"Yes. I'm fine."

He sighed. "I wanted you to experience everything, I still do. But now I know it's one step at a time."

"So let's move to the next step."

"Are you sure?"

"Yes." Imogen's pussy dampened—feeling his cock, even through their clothing, was a big turn-on. "It was too much, too fast," she said. "I wasn't prepared for it. I had no idea you'd do that to me, like that. I thought I'd be on the cross when you spanked me."

"So you've visualized it, in your head?"

"Yes. Of course." She tried to look nonchalant about her fantasy. About the thoughts that had swam through her mind when she'd had a quiet moment.

He smiled. "Then all is not lost."

"I hope not." Was it going to be all right? Yes, it was. Kane was an understanding, patient man, caring too. She wanted it to work between them, really she did.

He brushed his lips over hers. "Would you be willing? Now?"

She swallowed, heat continuing to flame over her face and her ass. "Willing for what?"

"Well, if it's the cross that's caught your attention, I needn't bother trying to sell you cages, wheels, and inversion tables."

"Yes," she said quietly and looking straight into his eyes. She had to be honest about what she wanted. He'd been honest, he'd laid his desires out on the table for her to see. "It's the cross."

He smiled, an I-got-what-I-wanted smile, and kissed her, his tongue stroking over hers and his mouth moving in a sensual dance.

Imogen ran her hands through his hair and down his back. This was more like it, kissing and cuddling, a hot man between her legs. She didn't think she'd ever be able to take discipline from a man, but sensual spanking, pain with arousal, that was a whole different ball game.

# CHAPTER THIRTEEN

Kane kissed her gently and sweetly for a long time. He ducked his head and suckled her nipples, teasing them to tight points with laps of his tongue and his hot mouth. He bit them too, just a little, just enough to make her squirm and gasp.

Eventually, he stood and looked down at her, the outline of his erection visible through his clothing.

"If you're willing," he said, pulling his shirt from the waistband of his trousers. "I'd like to strip you, harness you to the cross, and then show you how pain can mix with pleasure to produce outstanding orgasms."

"What an offer." Imogen watched as he peeled off his shirt, revealing his broad, taut chest and his defined abs.

"It's an offer I don't put on the table very often," he said, tossing the shirt next to a large red blanket.

"And why is that?" Imogen sat. Her buttocks were still tingling.

"Because I've found that the last few years I've become very selective about who I want to play with."

"And why is that... Sir?" Imogen touched her collar.

He smiled. "Because I want to connect emotionally, not just physically, when I play now." He took hold of the

137

zipper at the front of her outfit and slid it down to her navel.

The material gaped and loosened around her breasts.

"I want to connect with *you*," he whispered. "I want to get into your head, not just your body. I want to find out everything about you, even things you don't know."

A tremble ran up her spine. She wanted him to find out everything too. Take her to these places he'd promised.

"Yes," she said. "I want that too, Sir."

He pulled the zipper down to her crotch then kept on going, sliding it through her legs. "Stand."

She did.

He stepped around her and tugged the zipper upward from the other side, exposing the cleft of her ass.

Her pussy quivered and she was aware of dampness on her intimate folds.

Kane slipped his hand beneath the material and smoothed over her hot skin. "It will be perfect," he said. "Trust me."

"I do."

"So let's get started." He gripped the top of the outfit and eased it down her shoulders.

She helped the clinging fabric on its way and soon stood naked before him.

He smiled and took her hand, steered her to the cubicle with the free-standing cross.

She stared at the dark, polished wood as they approached. The manacles were made of black leather and had small silver chains. The center of the cross was padded and there was a small soft mat at its base.

"Like this," he said, moving in behind her. He clasped her right hand and lifted it up to the wrist harness.

His chest was warm and sexy against her back, and he'd pushed his hard-on to her ass, letting her know how much this was turning him on.

She watched as his nimble fingers secured the straps, then once it was tight, she let her arm relax, enjoying the way it was held in position.

He repeated the action with her left wrist, then stooped. She missed the feel of his body.

"Wider," he said, "much wider." He eased her feet to the base of the cross.

Cool air swirled over her damp pussy as her thighs parted. The vulnerability of the position became apparent, as did the fact she really was trapped.

She blew out a long, low breath as her ankles were secured. She could do this. This was what she wanted.

"Perfect," he said, coming to stand in front of her.

There'd be no squirming or struggling. She was securely fastened and her chest lodged against the center of the cross.

"I've fantasized about this moment," he said, stroking his fingers over her belly, dipping into her navel.

"I hope I live up to your expectations, Sir," she said, watching as he ran his tongue over his bottom lip.

"You already have." His touch traveled lower and he caressed her pussy lips, then stroked over her clit. "Are you turned on?"

"Yes... Sir."

"Good, because I sure as hell am." With his free hand, he cupped his cock through his trousers. "But this is all about you. It's your turn to have attention, *my* kind of attention." He circled her entrance and pushed in. "Squeeze my fingers."

She loved him penetrating her; she didn't have to be instructed to clench around his touch—it was what she wanted to do anyway. "Mmm..."

"Good girl," he said, gently pumping in and out. "Now hold that thought, there'll be more, but first a hit of endorphins. Go with it, don't fight it like you did before."

"Okay."

"Sir." There was a stern note in the word.

"Okay, Sir."

"I want you to let each bite of pain go to your pussy, just here..." He smoothed over her G-spot. "And just here." His thumb flicked over her clit.

Her abdominal muscles tensed and she yanked at the wrist harness. "Ohh…" she said. "Okay… Sir."

He smiled, pulled out, then moved from her view.

She wondered what he was getting. Would he use a paddle? A flogger? A whip? She had no idea.

Her rear end felt so exposed, hot too. She imagined it would already have a red glow.

"Now take a deep breath and hold it," he said, "and wait until I tell you to blow it out."

She did as he'd instructed and her chest swelled.

A sudden, searing sting slammed against her right buttock.

She bit her bottom lip and kept the breath in as the pain shot like fingers of fire over her skin. As that started to fade, a deeper, more dense pain traveled through her muscles.

"To your pussy," he said, "send it there as you blow out the breath."

She released the air with a puff and tried to focus on her pussy as he'd told her to.

Another burning slap.

It was the paddle, she was sure of it.

"Oh, God." She gritted her teeth. Was this what it was all about?

"That's it, perfect." He smoothed his hand over her heated skin. "You're doing so well. Now close your eyes and let your mind go blank. There is only me and you and the pain, nothing else exists."

She shut her eyes and was greeted with a firework display of colors dancing behind her lids.

He hit again.

She jerked. Her pussy was hot and swollen, her nipples tight. She wanted to get away from the pain, but then another strike bore down and she welcomed the new wave of sensation that layered over the other hits.

Something had switched.

She found herself looking forward to the next strike because each hit did indeed blast arousal straight to her cunt.

"Oh..."

"That's it." He stepped in front of her. He cupped her nape and kissed her.

She kept her eyes closed. She was spinning, giddy. She kissed him back but her mouth felt lazy.

"More?" he asked.

"Mmm..."

He gave it. Hard and fast. Hits that stung and burned, then powered through her body.

She moaned, long low gurgles that came up from her chest. She bucked backward then forward, trapped in a good way, because it meant she was getting what she needed.

A low buzzing noise wended its way into her brain.

The paddling had stopped.

"Let's see how this works for you," Kane said.

Imogen opened her eyes and lowered her head.

Kane held a long wand-like piece of kit with a domed white head. It was the head that was vibrating, shivering.

With his free hand, he parted her pussy lips.

A tremble of anticipation went through her. What was this?

"So pretty," he murmured as he placed the domed head against her clit.

"Oh, fuck..." she gasped, fighting all of her constraints in one frantic jerk. The wand was so intense and the sensation, straight over her clit, so raw.

"You're feeling it all now," he said. "Am I right?"

"It's... so much..." And it was; she was going to come.

"Ah, ah, ah... no orgasm until I say so."

She shut her eyes and thrust her hips as much as she could. There was no stopping her orgasm, the wand had claimed it. It was there, about to erupt.

Suddenly the sensation was gone.

She cried out at the loss. "Kane. Sir..." Oh, God, she'd just been about to...

He licked her bottom lip, tracing the outline. "It's not

time yet."

"It is…" she wailed.

He didn't reply, and before she could complain, the paddle connected with her sore ass.

"Ahh…" she cried, her clit throbbing and the pressure in her pussy screaming for release.

"Take it," he said, his voice calm, an exact contrast to the yelling in her head.

"Please…" she begged, clenching her fists so tight her nails dug into her palms. "Please, Kane… Sir…"

"Oh, good, the begging has started." He hit her again, a deft shot that took in both her buttocks on the underside.

"Ahhh."

The vibrations were suddenly back, her clit receiving heavenly stimulation.

"Oh, yes…" she said, pushing onto her toes. "That's it…"

Gone.

"No…" she yelped. "Please."

He hit her again.

Her pussy was so wet, the slickness was coating her folds.

She braced for more of the paddle. Took several hard *thwacks* and grunted each time the burn shot to her cunt.

The paddle suddenly landed on the floor with a clatter. Kane dropped to his knees in front of her, holding the wand.

"Please, Sir. I need to come…"

"I know." He touched the buzzing tip to her clit.

"More." It felt so good. She couldn't bear it if he moved it this time.

"Pardon?"

"More, Sir." She was floating, it was only the cross holding her down. Her mind spun, her body felt electrified. She was balancing on a precipice; she wanted to topple over, swirl into blissful climax and let it consume her. Never before had she felt so desperate to come, so focused on it.

Now it was all that mattered. All she could think about.

He pressed the wand more firmly over her clit.

She tensed her internal muscles as the pressure built with a ferocity that was almost frightening. She was on a short, swift climb to one hell of an orgasm.

He moved the wand.

"No…" she wailed, battling the cross. "It's too much. I need to…"

"So safe word." He held her hips still. "If it's too much."

"Will that… get me… a climax?" She was breathless.

"No, it will get you unfastened and dressed."

She groaned; that wasn't what she needed.

"Sweet Imogen," he said, kissing her mound. "Rest now and I'll give you what you want."

She opened her eyes. His shoulders were so wide and his biceps so thick and taut. The spotlight above highlighted the three stars on his torso and caught in his dark hair like sunshine would.

"Yes, oh, yes, Sir… that, please…"

He leaned forward, tongue out, and licked over her clit.

Her knees shook; a rattle went up her spine and ended in her teeth. This was it, what she needed.

She stared unblinking as Kane pressed his mouth to her pussy for the first time. He looked beautiful, his concentration alone enough to nearly tip her over the edge.

He released her hips and with his right hand pushed three long fingers into her pussy.

She was trapped, held hostage by the cross. She took what he gave.

"I'm… please…" she said, some part of her mind remembering she needed permission to let pleasure overflow. "Can I… Sir…?"

"Come," he said, his voice muffled because he was between her legs. "You may come now."

Her mouth fell open, her body stiffened, preparing for the onslaught of a wild orgasm. She held her breath, clenched her stomach. It was there… his tongue was wickedly good. He was finger-fucking her…

"Oh… oh…" she managed. "Argh… it's here…"

Her body seemed to explode and implode at the same time. Savage spasms racked her pussy and her clit pulsed against Kane's tongue. The cross creaked as her limbs fought it. Being so spread open, so available was as erotic as it was scary as Kane rode through her orgasm with her.

She clenched her ass cheeks, the sting of the paddle making itself known and firing new darts of pleasure over her skin.

On and on the bliss continued to ravage her and so did he. She'd never come so hard or had every sense so stimulated. It was new, scary, it was a high she'd never thought she'd reach.

"Kane," she sobbed.

"Baby." He lifted his mouth from her, rested his cheek on her belly and stroked her stinging ass with his free hand. "You did so well."

She was too out of breath to reply. He pussy was still clenching and releasing around his fingers.

"So perfect," he murmured, kissing her navel. "My perfect one."

She shut her eyes and let her head fall back—it suddenly seemed too heavy for her neck. A low gurgle of satisfaction rumbled up from her chest. She'd never felt so alive, her body so sated. He'd been right, everything else had faded away, it was only pain and pleasure and him. And being trapped as she'd climaxed, there'd been no escape from the ecstasy, it had been so concentrated.

He kissed his way up her body, only stopping when the cross got in his way. He kept his fingers lodged high, something for the aftershocks to tremble around.

Imogen remained out of breath for a minute or so. She shut her eyes and was happy to enjoy the aftermath and his touch. Every sense was heightened, her sex-smell strong, her flesh tingling.

"Breathe," he whispered against her ear and finally

pulling his fingers from her. "That's it, calm now..."

She concentrated on slowing her breaths.

Fiddling at her wrists told her she was being unshackled. She experienced a moment of sadness at that. Her time on the cross was over.

But it had been so good, so new.

She felt dreamy, almost out of her body, yet never so in it. As Kane released her final limb, her right ankle, her spine sagged.

"Hey, hey..." he said, scooping her up as though she was a damsel in distress. "I've got you."

"Mmm..." she mumbled, resting her head on his bare chest and hooking her arms around his neck.

"You need to rest," he said. "That was a hardcore first session."

She agreed but didn't have the energy to speak.

He carried her to the sofa, sat, then draped the soft blanket over her naked body.

His flesh was so warm and comforting. The smell of his skin and his stubbled chin as he pressed butterfly kisses to her head were all so perfect.

She let the dozy state overtake her. The flesh on her buttocks hurt but not in a bad way, in a lovely warm way. Her pussy was swollen and wet, her clit still tender.

"You did so well," he murmured. "My beautiful Imogen. I always knew you would. You're made for this, made for me..." He kissed her again, on the top of her head, then smoothed her hair.

Imogen nestled closer, she needed only him. He was her universe as she slipped between awake and asleep, conscious and not. He was her everything in that moment, an anchor, a savior.

"I've dreamed of this, having you in my arms, sated, sexy, sleepy," he said.

His voice sounded as if he were speaking underwater. Muffled and distant. Imogen was happy to be lulled by it and sank deeper into her dazed state.

"I feel like the luckiest man alive." He rubbed her shoulders over the blanket and held her tighter. "You're the ultimate prize," he whispered, "more than wealth, more than anything, I want you." He paused. "And I'm never going to let you go."

# CHAPTER FOURTEEN

Imogen had remained in the sleepy, almost drugged state for the rest of the evening. Kane had taken her back to the hotel and, after assisting her with a quick shower, he'd laid her on her stomach and applied soothing cream to her sore buttocks.

She'd taken the collar off just before she'd fallen into slumber, needing to be absolutely naked at his side.

But it was morning now, and as she poured tea from the breakfast trolley that had just been delivered to the suite, she'd never felt more awake. It was as though she'd had an injection of energy. She was excited about the future and ready for adventure. She also had a wonderfully sweet ache in her chest whenever she looked at Kane.

"How is your derrière, my dear?" he asked with a cheeky, bad-boy grin that didn't match how smart and important he looked in his Savile Row suit.

She rubbed her palm over the top of the toweling robe, caressing her right buttock. "Tender."

He adjusted the knot of his tie and knocked it slightly off center. "Is tender a problem?"

"I guess that depends on how much sitting down I have to do today."

"You can spend the day in bed, in the bath, lounging outside on the balcony in the sunshine or in the spa. You don't have to do anything."

"But I want to." She walked up to him and reached for his tie, straightened it.

He stared at her with a burning intensity in his eyes. "What do you want to do?"

"See the sights?" She drifted her hands over his lapels and brushed at an imaginary piece of fluff. "I haven't been here before, to New York. There's so much to see, other than sex clubs, that is."

"I can't argue with that." He reached for her hand and pressed his lips over her knuckles. "And once I've finished with these meetings I'm planning on rectifying that."

"Oh?"

"Yes. We're going to dinner with Taylor and Marie tonight in one of the most exclusive restaurants in the city."

"Yes, of course, and how wonderful." She'd forgotten about that.

"I hope you'll enjoy it, and afterwards I have a surprise for you."

"That sounds exciting."

"It will be."

"Does it involve getting naked?" She cocked her eyebrows and smiled. "My ass going red again?"

He chuckled. "My, oh my, you're a nymphomaniac now. One bite of the apple and you want it all."

Imogen shrugged with a grin still in place. "I just wondered. Not sure if my ass could take it two nights in a row."

"I have other plans for you and your sweet little ass tonight." He glanced at his watch. "But…"

"And what would that be?"

"But right now I have to go." He swept his lips over hers. "I'll be back here at six and we'll leave at seven."

"Okay, but what—?"

"I'll miss you." He stepped across the room and picked

up his phone. "In fact, I'm missing you already."

She hugged her arms around herself and watched him head to the elevator. She was melting inside. Her heart was beating for him, every single thing he said, did, she fell more in love. There was no denying it now. She had to face up to the facts.

Kane Ward wasn't the man she'd thought would light up her life—she never would have presumed to have a chance with him. But it seemed he'd chosen her to be his and she wasn't going to complain. Not when she felt like this, so on top of the world. Not when love had been absent from her life for so long and now it had raced into her world like a runaway train.

Imogen ate, then showered, and before long found herself heading down Fifth Avenue toward the public library. It was somewhere she'd wanted to go for a long time. Libraries always made her feel both in awe and inspired. So many words, so many thoughts all in one place and all tangible and within reach. And this one, in New York, she'd seen it in movies and documentaries. The beautiful building was as much a draw as the books.

She wandered past the huge stone lions that guarded the entrance, up the wide stone steps, and through the enormous pillars into the lobby. Instantly, the hustle and bustle of the street faded and cool air surrounded her. It had been hot outside, noisy too, but in here it was as though a cloak of calm had been thrown over her shoulders and the lighting became muted, less harsh for her eyes.

A small rectangular brochure sat on a long, polished reception desk. Behind it, two women, heads bowed as though concentrating on computer screens, sat quietly side by side.

"May I?" Imogen asked.

"Sure, go ahead," one said without looking up.

Imogen reached for the slim visitors' guide, then glanced at a stern-looking security man standing to her left. She gave him a brief smile, then opened up the map and stared around the vacuous space.

"Wow," she said quietly.

Two huge sets of steps led upward and arches beneath them appeared to feed into more corridors. She decided to head up and enjoy the view from there. She wished Kane had come with her—he would have liked it. Crowds didn't work for him, but there were no crowds here.

She glanced through an open doorway. A long room, walls stacked high with books, greeted her. In the center of the room, sitting at heavy wooden tables, people of all ages and colors had their heads bent over books and piles of papers. Some held pens and were either writing furiously or fiddling, chewing on them. Others were deep in concentration. A few stood by the shelves and one man was halfway up a ladder reaching for a fat leather-bound volume.

She stepped into the silence. Just the sound of her soft shoes on the wooden floor seemed super loud. She wondered what type of books were in this room and wandered up to a stacked shelf to her right. The title of the first book she settled her gaze on was *The History of Chemical Engineering*—not something she could sit with and soak up the atmosphere.

She wandered to the next section, heading deeper into the room. A librarian, sitting at a desk on a plinth, glanced her way. Imogen half smiled, then reached for a book and pulled it from the shelf. *Anthropological Debates*. Not quite her thing either. She put it back.

A sudden loud beeping rang around the room.

She gasped.

*Shit.*

It was her phone.

She tore at the zipper on her purse and pulled it out, which only made the second beep—signaling she had a text message—all the louder.

"Sorry," she mouthed at the librarian, who had stood and wore a furious frown. "Really sorry."

Quickly, she flicked the phone to silent and hurried past

a table of what appeared to be school students who were all staring at her.

A flush traveled up her throat to her cheeks. She sped up, fled through the doorway onto the main landing that looked down at the reception area. Her face felt on fire.

Damn it! Why hadn't she thought to turn off the sound on her phone? She always did if she was going into meetings or somewhere silent. How could she have forgotten? It must be because she was in holiday mode.

Holiday? It had been a business trip to start out with. When had it become a holiday?

She pressed her fingers over her hot cheeks and sat on a bench. She hoped the librarian wouldn't chase out after her and order her from the building.

She glanced at the screen on her phone.

*Message from master*

"Message from master?" she whispered. "What the…?" She hit open.

*My darling Imogen. I hope you are having a nice day. As I predicted, I miss you.*

It was Kane, obviously. But when had he put his personal cell number in her phone?

*Hello, Kane,* she wrote. *When did you get your hands on my phone?*

*When you were sleeping last night. And you forgot Sir in your text.*

*I'm not wearing the collar. That means you're Kane.* She hit send and stared out of an arched window at the busy Manhattan street that led into the distance.

*Maybe one day you'll wear the collar permanently.*

She reread the text. That was a pretty heavy thing to suggest. It seemed almost like marriage but with a twist. She put the phone in her bag and pulled out a bottle of water, took a sip.

A few minutes later she got another message. She put the lid back on her water and took out the phone again.

*Where are you?*

*At the library and you nearly got me thrown out. I forgot to switch to silent. If looks could kill I'd be dead.*

*Silly girl. Would you like me to hire the place? So you can have it to yourself?*

*I don't think that will be necessary. Where are you?*

*In a meeting with a sheik, an ambassador, and eight company directors.*

*And you're texting?*

*They're talking amongst themselves.*

She smiled. He was bad, but she loved that he was sitting in a boardroom thinking of her, texting her.

*Last night was amazing.* She grinned as she hit send.

*I agree.*

She hesitated then, *I've never come so hard. You took my breath away.*

*I'm glad to hear it.*

*My ass is still sore. I'm sitting down now. I can feel the paddle on my skin.*

*Good.*

*What did I look like to you, when I was on the cross?*

*Sexy.*

*Is that all?*

*Sexy, vulnerable, beautiful… mine.*

*Yours?*

*Yes, all mine.*

Imogen licked her lips. She liked being all his and she could almost hearing him say the word 'mine' in a low, growling voice.

*Did you feel satisfied after I came on your tongue?* Again she hit send, knowing that she was pushing the risqué nature of the texts.

*You're a little minx and you'll pay for this!*

*Pay for what?* She squirmed on the seat and her tender skin complained. She knew exactly what she was doing and it sounded like it was working.

*You know what…*

*Are you hard… Master?*

*You know damn well I am. How could I not be thinking of you on the cross, surrendered to me, willing to let me show you my ways?*

*Your ways seem to be agreeing with me.*

*Well, be prepared for more, later.*

She grinned and her belly clenched. She could hardly wait. *I have to go.*

*Send me a photograph… now.*

*Okay.*

Imogen stood and glanced around. She saw a sign for the restrooms and hurried toward it. Once inside a cubicle, she stripped off her top, then her bra. The cubicle wall was wooden, the same rich nutty shade as the bookshelves. Quickly, she fluffed her hair and licked her lips. She angled the phone and took a selfie.

Damn. The picture looked shocking with the flash.

She reposed and took another without. Much better—her skin was flesh-colored, her nipples rosy. Her hair tumbled down around her shoulders in a just-fucked way, and she'd pouted a little as she'd concentrated on taking the picture.

She saved it, then hit send to master. The small mailing sign seemed to take forever to travel over the top of the screen, but finally it went.

*Sheik Mohammed says I'm a very lucky man.*

"Ahh…" Imogen slapped her hand over her mouth. No, he wouldn't have, surely. It was for his eyes only. Really? Oh, God, this would be terrible if it got out or got back to her superiors at Coutts. How could she have been so impulsive? She shook her head and frowned.

*Please hit delete on that photo!*

*I'll do no such thing. But don't worry, the sheik hasn't seen it. He thinks I'm checking the stock exchange, not looking at hot pictures of my half-naked woman and deciding what to do to her tonight.*

*Thank goodness for that.*

*But I really should voice my opinion on the takeover. I will see you later. Be ready.*

*Yes, Sir.*

*And now I really can't stand up to make my point. Goodbye, tease.*

Imogen slipped her phone away and put her clothes back on. She'd never sent indecent images of herself before, not to anyone, yet here she was flashing pictures of her breasts to Kane Ward.

Bloody hell. Her life had turned upside down. This time last week she was running a bank and working all the hours she was awake. Now she was in New York with a tender ass, sending lewd pictures and wondering what kinky things one of the richest men in the country was going to do to her later.

She put her hair back in its ponytail to keep the air flowing around her hot neck. It seemed Kane Ward was pushing her boundaries in more ways than one, and as he'd promised, letting out a side of her she hadn't known was there.

• • • • • •

After a pleasant walk around Central Park and an ice cream, Imogen went back to the hotel. She poured a drink from the minibar and spent a relaxed hour enjoying the view over the city and painting her toe- and fingernails a deep shade of scarlet. She'd was planning on wearing her little black dress to dinner and the red would brighten up the outfit, plus it would match her lipstick.

She had a long soak in the bath—with a whole bottle of bubbles tipped in—then dried, applied body cream, and put on sexy black underwear. In just her knickers and bra, she sat at the dressing table and began to pile up her hair with pins. She hummed a gentle tune, something she'd heard back home, and enjoyed the process of preparing herself for Kane.

She wondered what his brother would be like. Would he have the same determined, masterful air that Kane exuded, or would he be meeker, the shier, younger brother always looking up to his older sibling? It would be nice to meet him and his... girlfriend. Yes, girlfriend, not wife, that's what Kane had said, wasn't it?

Imogen had just pulled on the tight-fitting but elegant black dress when she heard the elevator door. She was about to struggle with the zipper at the back of the dress but waited, hoping for help. "Is that you, Kane?" she called, her heart giving a happy flip that she'd see him any second.

"You look beautiful," he said, coming into the room.

"Thank you." She smiled.

He didn't look bad himself—his suit still pristine and not a hair out of place. His appearance was the same as when he'd left that morning.

"Do you need a hand with that?" He nodded at where she was now fumbling with the zip.

"Yes, please." She turned, offering him her back.

He took the zipper and touched his lips to the patch of skin between her shoulder and neck.

"Though after that little messaging performance and then the picture," he said, his breaths hot on her flesh, "I should really be tipping you over my knee and spanking you."

The skin on her buttocks tingled. Getting tipped over his knee at the club hadn't worked for her, but now... now she knew what it could lead to...

"Except you're not wearing the collar, so I won't." He dragged the zipper upward and the material tightened around her chest. "Will you wear it later though?"

"The collar?"

"Yes."

She turned and rested her hands on his upper arms. "If that's what you want."

"It's the start of what I want." He cupped her chin and kissed her.

Imogen sighed and rested against him. The day had seemed to double in hours as she'd waited for this moment.

"Mmm, so good," he said, pulling back. "Too good, in fact." He glanced at his watch. "But there is no time for any of that now... much as I would like there to be after today."

"What do you mean?"

"I don't think I've ever had to address a boardroom full of CEOs and dignitaries while sitting down."

"Why?" She knew why, but wanted him to say it. She pressed her lips together to hold in a satisfied smile.

"Because." He took her hand and rested it over his groin. His cock was solid and pushing at his trousers. "Once I'd seen that photograph I was ready to go. Still am."

"I'm sorry."

He grinned. "No, you're not, but it's okay. I'll get my revenge."

A small tremble wound up Imogen's spine. The sparkle in his eyes, the feel of his erection, and the way his breaths had picked up, just a little, turned her on. She had no doubt he'd get his revenge and it would be as sweet as it was torture.

He suddenly stepped away. "I'll shower and we'll go. Give me five minutes."

"Okay."

He disappeared into the other bedroom where his clothes were and he'd showered previously.

Imogen reapplied her lipstick that had become smudged by his kiss, and added the pretty sapphire necklace and earrings to her outfit.

The night stretched ahead, full of possibilities and adventure—full of Kane.

# CHAPTER FIFTEEN

Imogen sipped her wine and looked across the table at Taylor and Marie. She'd been right to think Taylor would be like his brother; he was. Maybe a fraction taller and a little leaner, but other than that he had similar features, the same dark hair, and a way of moving that screamed control in every aspect of his life.

Marie, on the other hand, was soft and pretty and quick to smile. She had gentle curves and generous breasts and wore a pale blue dress that accentuated her enviable hourglass figure. Her blond hair fell like bubbles around her shoulders, and when she moved her head to talk to Taylor, the slim leather collar around her neck shifted slightly against the tendons.

A week ago, Imogen would have thought it an unusual necklace, but now she knew differently. Taylor and Marie were clearly a part of the BDSM scene.

"So how is it going with the new club project?" Taylor asked, directing his question to Kane.

"Good." Kane picked up his knife, then began to spread foie gras on a slice of wheat bread. "And I'm moving forward to acquiring the properties in Berlin and Rome. The one in London is already a done deal."

Imogen cut into her salmon terrine. He was talking about the sex clubs he was setting up, he must be. They were the cities he'd said he was buying in. It was clear Taylor was in the know about the project.

"And Imogen is helping me out with details," Kane added. "We went last night."

"Oh, really?" Taylor asked. "How did that go, Imogen?"

Imogen looked quizzically at Kane. What did he mean her to reveal? That they'd played and she'd been tied to the cross and paddled? That it had been the hottest, edgiest sexual experience of her life and she'd been practically knocked unconscious with the force of her orgasm?

"She has a good eye," Kane said, "for what's appealing to women."

"I'm sure." Taylor popped a prawn in his mouth and chewed. When he'd swallowed, he spoke again. "Actually, I meant to ask you a favor about that club, Kane."

"You want a recommendation?" Kane asked.

"How did you guess?" Taylor laughed. "Yes, we're here to stay for a while." He brushed a lock of hair over Marie's shoulder and his face softened into a loving smile. "Marie is planning on setting up a fashion design business, so it would be good to have somewhere to play that's local."

"Other than in my apartment?" Kane laughed.

"I'm sorry about that." Taylor shrugged, not appearing sorry in the least. "I'll start searching for somewhere else so you can have your place back when you're in town."

"No, don't worry about it. It would be empty most of the time. I'm only here a few weeks a year. I'd rather you used it."

"Appreciate it."

"And of course I'll put your names forward," Kane said. "I can't see it being a problem."

"Thank you," Marie said, smiling and touching the collar for what seemed like the hundredth time.

"My pleasure," Kane said, "and I should say it's very beautiful, your collar."

"Thank you." Marie turned to Taylor.

He leaned close to her and pressed a quick kiss to her lips. "We chose it today."

"Congratulations," Kane said. "I didn't realize it was so new."

"Yes, I love it. Rubies are my favorite." She stroked over the small red stones set in the thin leather. "I'm going to wear it always."

"You'll never take it off?" Imogen asked, the words coming out with more surprise lacing them than she'd planned.

"No," Marie said. "Taylor is my master. I am his woman." She sucked in a breath, her chest straining against her dress. "This collar is a symbol of my commitment to him and that I will obey him at all times."

"At all times?" Imogen struggled with that. How could they have an equal relationship if Taylor always told Marie what to do and she did it? Not just in the bedroom but also out of it, in everyday life?

"I'm sorry," Taylor said, glancing at his brother. "I thought... we thought, with the club and everything that..."

"That Imogen was part of our lifestyle," Kane finished for him. "She's new, but a quick learner."

"I'm sorry," Imogen said, worried that she'd said something wrong. "If I offended you."

Marie smiled. "No apology needed, and I'm glad you're learning about the way we live and intend to live—there are many ways for relationships to work, not just the traditional one."

"Yes, I'm seeing that."

"Marie knows that I will only make decisions that put her first," Taylor said, topping up everyone's wine. "It is my responsibility as her master to make sure she is happy and satisfied in every aspect of her life and can have room to be the best person she can be and achieve her goals."

"I understand that and it's very honorable," Imogen said, "but what if you disagree on something basic, like the color to paint the bathroom, or where to go for your holiday, whether to have red or white wine?" She indicated the glass of Merlot in front of her.

"We wouldn't," Marie said.

"But what if—?"

"We wouldn't," Marie repeated. "Because the decisions are Taylor's to make and I know he'll have made them in my best interest."

"But—?"

"Imogen, try this foie gras," Kane said, hovering a tiny triangle of bread by her mouth. "It's delicious."

Imogen hesitated, then took the morsel of food Kane had offered.

"How is it?" Kane asked.

"Mmm, nice." Imogen wiped at a crumb from the corner of her mouth.

"Tell me about your fashion designing," Kane said to Marie.

Marie glanced at Taylor, then smiled. "I've been designing for as long as I can remember, but it's a very hard business to get into. Taylor has some ideas, though."

Imogen swallowed the foie gras, then drank a mouthful of wine. It was clear Kane didn't want the conversation to continue about Taylor and Marie's relationship. Was that because he didn't want her to offend them, or because he hoped for her to be just like Marie one day and do everything she was told… by him?

She sat back and listened as the conversation moved from Marie's design plans to a location for her new office in Manhattan. Taylor was positive and supportive and keen for Marie to make a success of her new business. Imogen was pleased for her; she'd found a man to love and the future was exciting. She could imagine being friends with Marie; she had a warmth about her.

But could she be friends with someone who thought so differently? Who was happy to obey a man all day, every day?

Taylor appeared as in love with Marie as she was him. He touched her frequently, looked at her every few seconds, and fussed over whether she had enough water and wine and if her food was to her liking.

Imogen studied Taylor's hands. They were big, like his brothers, with neat nails and a faint coating of hair just sneaking past his cuffs. Did he use his hands on Marie the way Kane had on her—slapping, wielding instruments of pain, withholding orgasm? Did he use his strong fingers to tie ropes, insert plugs, vibrators? How often did he bind his collared woman onto a cross, or a bench for flogging and fucking and…?

"Imogen…"

"Mmm, sorry." Imogen realized Kane was speaking to her. She smiled.

"Your main course."

"Oh, yes, lovely." She glanced at the waiter at her side, who held her coq au vin. "Thank you."

He set down the meal.

"This looks delicious," she said.

"It does," Marie said. "It's awesome here, don't you think, Imogen?"

"Yes, stunning." Imogen nodded and took in the elegant restaurant around her.

The walls were a mixture of wooden panels and black glass. Huge candelabras dangled from the ceiling and several portraits in golden frames hung on the walls. Each table was set far enough apart from the next for privacy, and the waiters appeared to glide silently around the customers, blending with the background.

"Is this your first time in New York?" Marie asked, tucking into her own meal.

"Yes, it is."

"Have you seen the sights?"

"Well, not much." She glanced at Kane, who was cutting into his steak. "I went to the library today, though."

"Oh, it's beautiful," Marie said, then sighed. "I've spent

several afternoons there flicking through the vintage design books. So peaceful."

"Well, it was until Imogen arrived," Kane said, chuckling.

Imogen felt her cheeks redden again just at the memory of her phone disturbing the tranquility.

"Why, what happened?" Taylor asked.

"I forgot to switch my phone to silent," Imogen said with a sigh.

Taylor laughed.

Marie pulled a sympathetic face.

"Yes," Kane said. "Inappropriate texts can be very distracting, can't they?"

Imogen glared at him. Surely he wasn't going to reveal...

He leaned close and touched the back of his fingers to her cheek and stroked down her face. "But I'm not complaining." He pressed his lips to hers.

"Oh, get a room," Taylor said, smiling.

"Huh, you can't talk," Kane said, glancing at his brother. "You've hardly been able to keep your hands off your woman." He winked at Marie. "Not that I blame you."

Taylor shrugged. "You're right, I can't help myself. Maybe I'll let you play with her one day, at the club."

Kane reached for his napkin and coughed.

Taylor's smile dropped a fraction. "Ah, okay, so how is your chicken, Imogen?"

Imogen looked at him, then at Kane. "Fine, l mean beautiful." What had he meant by play with her? Did he mean he'd let Kane flog Marie? Fuck Marie? Did they do that, the brothers?

Bloody hell! One thing was for sure, the Wards were not only unimaginably rich and devastatingly handsome, they were also kinky as fuck and it seemed they had made BDSM their hobby.

• • • • • • •

The end of the meal arrived, and after lots of goodbyes, Taylor and Marie took a cab and Kane's limo pulled up at the kerb to collect them.

Imogen slid onto the soft seat and rested her purse on her lap.

Kane sat next to her.

"Are we going back to the hotel?" she asked as the driver steered out into the traffic.

Kane took her left hand and placed it between both of his. "No. I have a surprise for you."

"Oh, what is it?"

"Well, I feel responsible for the fact you haven't seen as many of the sights that you would have liked to. I'm hoping this will go some way to rectifying that."

"You don't need to feel like that. I've had a lovely time. And it was great to meet your brother and Marie. They were really nice company."

"I'm glad you think so." He raised her hand and kissed her fingertips that were peeking out from between his. "Even if their way of living is a little confusing for you."

She hesitated. "Yes, it is a bit."

"You can't understand why a strong woman would be willing to hand herself over so completely to a man."

"I think that's it basically. Marie seems to be very capable, intelligent—why does she need Taylor to make the most basic decisions for her?"

"She doesn't need him to, she wants him to. That's the difference."

Imogen thought about it. "Okay, but why does she *want* him to?"

"Because she loves him. It's a way of showing him how much she trusts him in and out of the bedroom. It's a great honor for Taylor to have Marie wear his collar twenty-four-seven."

"But isn't it hard for her to live normally when she has to run everything by her master?"

"It's only between them, this arrangement. She's her

own person with thoughts and opinions, talents too, I'm sure." He paused. "It takes a strong person to submit, Imogen. It's not for the weak or the faint of heart."

She was quiet.

"As you proved last night." He lowered his voice and leaned a little closer. "It took guts to allow me to tie you to that cross and paddle your ass. There is nothing easy about handing yourself or your pain and pleasure to another person. I admire anyone at peace enough with themselves to do that."

"Thank you, I think."

He smiled a little, then pointed out of the window. "We're here."

"Where?" She looked at the pedestrians rushing past.

"You'll see."

The driver hopped out and opened the door. Imogen stepped onto the sidewalk and stared upward. They were directly beneath the Empire State Building.

It stretched on and on, higher and higher, piercing the night sky. The top section was lit with bright red spotlights and appeared to glow.

"Mr. Ward?" A man in a suit and bowler hat stepped from the entrance of the building.

"Yes." Kane nodded and took Imogen's hand.

"This way, sir." The man used an outstretched arm to hold the door open.

Imogen was tugged forward, away from the press of New Yorkers who were dodging around them. Kane moved fast, clearly not liking being on the sidewalk.

Like the library, the lobby of the Empire State Building was silent, majestic, and huge.

"Is it open?" Imogen asked. "It doesn't seem it." There didn't appear to be any staff around or indeed any other tourists.

"It is for us," Kane said, slipping his hand around her waist. "Come on, we're going to the top. I did tell you I'd take you there."

He had indeed—in the car, on the way from the airport to the hotel.

They followed the man who'd greeted them to a set of elevators with shiny brass doors. He hit the button on the first one. When it opened, he bobbed his head. "Everything is as you requested, Mr. Ward. Have a nice time."

"Thank you," Kane said, steering Imogen into the elevator.

The doors shut with a soft swoosh, leaving them alone. Imogen looked at the round black buttons—one hundred and two.

"It's a clear night," Kane said. "We should have a great view."

Imogen felt her tummy lurch as they were zoomed upward. "It's very high."

"It is the best spot to see New York from, so I'm told."

"Have you been here before?"

"Only to meetings, never past the seventy-first floor."

"So it's a new experience for both of us."

"It is."

The elevator slowed and a small digital sign announced they were at the observation deck.

"Are you okay?" Kane asked when she hesitated before stepping out.

"Yes, of course." She wouldn't let vertigo bother her. She could do this.

She headed into the corridor. "There really is no one else here," she said.

"No, of course not. I wanted us to have it all to ourselves." He glanced left then right. "This way."

The tiled floor was art deco style and the sound of her heels echoed around the wide space. Several big black-and-white photographs on the walls showed images of the building under construction.

They reached a set of glass doors. The night sky lay beyond but none of the usual New York lights. They were too high for that.

The doors slid open. The first thing Imogen noticed as she stepped onto the viewing platform was a mass of red roses. There were dozens of pedestals set almost in a circle around her, full of long-stemmed roses. Some were still buds but many were open and at their most beautiful.

She breathed deep, the powdery, sweet scent filling her lungs and mixing with the night air.

"Do you like?" Kane asked, settling his gaze on her.

"Well, yes... but... who...?"

"They're for you, of course. I thought you'd enjoy red roses." He glanced at the top point of the building that was also glowing red. "You like red, don't you? I often see you wearing it."

"Well, yes. But..."

"Tonight," he said, reaching for her and pulling her close, "the Empire State Building glows red, just for you, Imogen, at my request, and to show you how much you mean to me."

"You mean... you did this? The red all over this building that can be seen by millions of people?"

"Of course."

"And the roses, but there are so many... I can't take them all home." She surveyed the forest of flowers. She noticed now the black pedestals they stood on were placed over a large red carpet sprinkled with more petals.

"They're not to take home," he said, tracing her jawline with the tip of his finger. "They're just to enjoy now, while we're here. They're romantic."

"They're extravagant." She slipped from his arms and went up to the nearest bunch, stroked over a petal.

"Extravagant," he said with a flippant huff. "I haven't even started yet, Imogen. This is just so you'll always remember your first trip to the top of this iconic building."

"Well, I certainly will." She turned to him.

A small breeze rustled through the flowers and shifted a strand of hair over his forehead.

She walked up to him and brushed it aside. "And you

hired the place…?"

"Only this floor." He shrugged. "Though if you'd rather I had the building emptied I'm sure that can be arranged." He went to reach for his phone.

"No, no." She laughed. "It's fine. It's more than fine." She gestured around, smiling. "Perfect."

"Come on, look at the view, that's one of the things we're here for." He stepped away and lifted two full champagne flutes from a silver tray. "Here."

"Champagne as well."

"Of course."

She took a sip. Thoughts of the height she was at and how tiny everything down below would appear when she looked over the edge left her mind. What else were they up here for? She hardly dared ask. Kane Ward had taken her by surprise too many times. Perhaps she should, though, just get it out into the open.

She walked to the outer barrier that was encased with a cage-like fence, and stared at New York stretching in front of her. A large, dense square of blackness told her she was looking in the direction of Central Park.

She sucked in a deep breath. Yes, she was very high.

"It's beautiful," he said. "Just like you." He touched the rim of his glass to hers and took a sip.

She did the same, then twirled the stem in her fingers. "What else are we here for? Other than the view, that is."

He smiled and nodded. "Patience really isn't your strong point, is it?"

"Maybe curiosity is a more powerful force."

"Perhaps." He took her glass and set it aside, placed his down too.

"This seems serious," she said, wondering what was going on.

"It is. I've waited a long time for this."

Another gust of wind slipped past them. Imogen shivered as it struck her shoulders and filtered through her silky dress.

"Here." Quickly, he shrugged out of his jacket and wrapped it around her, letting the arms hang loose.

"Thank you." His body heat seeped onto her skin like an embrace, the material big and heavy, comforting too.

"Imogen," he said, moving up close. "From that first moment I saw you, nearly two years ago, you've filled my thoughts."

"I have?" Really? She'd filled his thoughts?

"Yes." He gave a small huff. "I don't really need to make appointments every few months to see my bank manager. I have people who work for me who can do that."

"Well, I did think it a little odd. Your reasons for visiting always concerned matters your accountants could have handled quite easily."

"I know, and I'm sorry if that was shallow of me."

"Not at all." She paused. "I looked forward to your visits. Very much."

"I'm glad." He rubbed his hands down to her elbows, then up again to her shoulders. "But my life, the business I'm in, it's crazy. Even finding the time to fantasize about you was in short supply. There is always so much going on. Somewhere to be, someone to see, a deal to close."

"You fantasized about me?" A thrill shot through her.

He lowered his voice to a husky murmur. "You know damn well I did and I've already confessed that."

She swallowed. What themes had his sexy thoughts taken? What had she been wearing, what he'd been doing to her? Did reality live up to the fantasy?

"My problem is not just time," he said. "As you now know, I have flavors other than vanilla that yank my chain. They're there, I can't remove them. It's like they've been hardwired into me."

She nodded.

"So not only was it hard finding the time and the opportunity to get you to myself, I knew once I did I also had to put my kinks on the table to see if you'd take the bait."

"Okay…"

He frowned. "I had to work up to that. What if you'd walked away from that BDSM club thinking I was a pervert? What if you'd demanded to be flown back to the UK and switched to another branch of Coutts so I could never see you again? What if you'd gone to the papers?"

"Kane, that wouldn't happen." She pressed her hand over his cheek. She hated to see him so worried. "And I don't think you're a pervert, not at all."

"Good, because I'm not. I just enjoy BDSM and all that it entails. I'm not the only one, as you've seen."

Imogen glanced to her right and stared at the silvery lights dotted over a tall square building.

"Which brings me to the last stage of my seduction of you," he said.

"Seduction? Stages?" She looked back at him. "You sound like you planned it all."

"I did. I'm a businessman; it's how my mind works."

"In every aspect of your life?"

"Yes. I don't accept failure and that means ensuring plans run smoothly and being in control of the outcome."

She was quiet for a moment, then, "Tell me more."

"I've made sure every step of the process of making you mine is at the lowest risk of failing. The date at the races— you thought that was business, you couldn't refuse to join me."

"I also thought the trip here was business."

"I think you rumbled me pretty quickly." He shrugged, just a little, and his white shirt pressed against his torso. "But I couldn't help myself in the car when you flashed your stocking. I'd been waiting too long."

"You couldn't wait but you're not sorry about the deception, are you?"

"No, it was a means to an end."

"And what is the end of your plan, Mr. Ward? What will measure your success? Because I think it's safe to say you have already seduced me and in ways I never would have thought possible."

"I haven't quite conquered you yet," he said, "there is still more to achieve."

"Which is?"

"Us. Together. I know it's been quick while we've been here, the transition from client and bank manager to lovers. But you can't deny there has been chemistry between us for a long time. It just needed room to breathe."

"I'm not denying it." She stared into his dark eyes. Was he suggesting what she thought he was? Something long term between them? "And yes, giving it room to breathe has been wonderful."

"So you'll think about it?"

"What? Think about what?"

He cupped her cheeks. "Being mine. Wearing my collar."

She stared into his handsome face. She wanted nothing more than to be his and for him to be hers. But the collar…?

"The collar," she said, then paused and took a deep breath. She had to be true to herself and what felt right for her, at this moment in time at least. "I'll wear it in the bedroom or in a scene. Any more than that is too much for me to handle right now."

"Okay. Okay." He nodded. "I get that. I'm sorry to push it. I've always wanted more of everything and I guess that includes you."

"It's just too much, I'm still getting used to this whole BDSM thing." She paused. "There's lots for me to learn, I get that, about myself and us too."

"But you're willing to try to understand, which means we'll make it work, Imogen. I know we will." He gathered her close.

"Yes, we will, and being yours is exactly what I want to be."

"Thank the Lord for that." He smiled, then pressed his mouth to hers.

She melted against him. Her heart swelled. She was in

love with a wonderful, exciting, vibrant man, and the future held so much promise. She was high, not just physically by being on top of the Empire State Building, but also emotionally. She felt like she could fly. Soar above the skyscrapers, take the whole world on. Happiness was a good feeling, and she'd do everything she could to ensure it stayed.

# CHAPTER SIXTEEN

Imogen took one red rose back to The Four Seasons hotel and set it on the piano. The red petals were stunning next to the shiny black wood.

"Are you tired?" Kane asked, removing the slim tie he'd worn with his suit, then undoing the top button of his shirt.

"No." She studied him. Thoughts of going to sleep couldn't be further from her mind. She had a hot man now. Someone who could take her to wonderful places and play her body like a musical instrument—why would she want to sleep?

"Good, because I have plans for you."

"That sounds interesting."

"It is." He removed his shirt so that he was bare-chested.

Imogen's mouth watered at the sight of his sun-kissed skin and the three stars inked onto his flesh. She wanted to touch him, lick him, feel his body pushing up against hers—pushing into hers.

He walked over to her and stooped. He carefully removed her shoes the way he had her boots that first night.

She stared at the top of his head and watched the tendons in his shoulders shift as he moved.

He straightened, towering over her now that she'd lost

her heels. "This way." He linked their fingers and tugged her to the room he'd used earlier to shower and change.

When he opened the door, Imogen paused.

This bedroom was quite different to the one she'd been using. The walls were painted a darker shade and the drapes at the window were black. The bed had silky gray sheets and pillows, and two lamps with burgundy shades gave the room a sultry glow.

Standing in the middle of the room was a padded leather bench. It was like the one she'd seen at the club. The first night she'd witnessed it in use, the submissive had been tied, spanked, and fucked as she lay over it.

She glanced at Kane.

He tilted his chin and his eyes narrowed.

That was him feeling vulnerable, she knew that now. He was showing her something that was very personal to him, yet trying to act like it didn't matter.

It did.

"You've been busy," she said. "Planning."

"I told you, I plan everything."

"So you do." She stepped away from him and ran her fingertip over the cool black leather on the bench. She couldn't deny that she was excited to see it. She'd thought of it several times. After the cross it was the piece of apparatus she was the most interested in.

The door to the room clicked shut.

At the side of the bench, a mirror had been leaned against the wall. It was huge, eight feet by eight feet, and perfect for whoever was on the bench to turn to the side and see their reflection.

Imogen stepped around the head section, tracing her fingers over the stitching. A table had been set next to the bench. It held a small brown leather bag and one long length of slim black rope.

She looked at Kane. He was standing with his arms at his sides, his jaw was set tight, and he was studying her with an intensity that made her insides quiver.

"Is this for...?" She held up the rope and the end slithered to the floor.

"Shibari, yes."

"You want to tie me up?"

"Yes."

"Like the girls in the pictures at the club."

"Yes."

"Can I ask one question?"

"Of course." He folded his arms with his hands tight beneath his armpits and his biceps flexed against his knuckles.

"Why? What do you get from it?"

"What do I get from it?" He sounded incredulous.

"Yes."

"I get to see you with my ropes over your beautiful skin. I get to have you, totally, as mine. Not just your body but your mind, your soul. You'll have to trust me, work with me, hand yourself over to me, that's what I get—you."

"Okay." Her stomach did an excited flip. She really was the center of this show.

He relaxed his arms and went up to the bench. He pressed his palm over the end. "One of my fantasies, when I first saw you..."

"Go on." This was something she wanted to hear.

"Was to have you bound and tipped forward on a bench like this. I thought for a long time about the types of knots I wanted to use, how to position your breasts, your arms, your legs." He paused. "Then I spent a lot of time thinking about what I'd do to you once you were like that." He stared straight at her. "Tied up and helpless."

"What would you do?" Her throat felt dry, her heart was racing.

He was silent for a moment, then, "I'd rather show you."

Imogen looked at the bench, then the ropes. She switched her attention to the bag, wondering what was in there.

"Please," he said with an uncharacteristic note of

pleading in his voice.

A tug of longing ran from her clit to her pussy and her nipples spiked. She'd been fascinated by the pictures on the walls at the club and now Kane wanted to strap her up like that—more than wanted to, he was desperate to.

"Okay," she said, flexing, then unflexing her fingers. "As long as the safe word will get me released."

"Absolutely, within seconds. It always will, no matter what." He nodded, then smiled. "But you won't want to use it."

"Okay, Sir." She glanced at her feet. "Thank you, Sir."

She was aware of him moving past her to the bag that sat on the table to her left. He opened it and took something out. Then he was behind her, undoing the zipper of her dress. It loosened and fell away.

Her underwear was dark and sexy but didn't stay on long. Kane efficiently removed her bra, then had her step out of her knickers.

"And this," he said, undoing the clasp on her necklace. "Pretty as it is about your neck, it has to go." He set it aside, the metal producing a delicate tinkle as he lay it down on the surface.

He slipped his hands over her shoulders, his forearms brushing her ears. He held the collar between his fingers as if showing it to her. "Do you consent to wearing my collar?"

"Yes." Her voice was breathy, excited. She found that she wanted to wear the collar. She understood clearer now what it meant. She was safe in that collar; it was a sign of her willing submission to the man she loved.

He fastened it, carefully checking it wasn't too tight.

"You're beautiful," he said, kissing her shoulder. "Look at yourself in the mirror."

She raised her head and was greeted with the image of her naked self—naked except for the collar, which looked all the more startling with her hair piled high.

"Everything about you," he said, slipping his hands around her body and cupping her breasts, "is exquisite.

Under those suits all that time, you were hiding this from me." He pinched her nipples, pulling them taut.

She released a long, low breath. Dampness was growing between her legs. She wanted to get started and find out exactly what he had in store for her.

"You must stand very still," he said. "While I harness you in my ropes. You should put your hands behind your back now."

"Yes, Sir."

"And I want you to watch in the mirror, very carefully, so you see how prettily I bind my ties around your body."

"Yes, Sir."

He reached for the rope. The end trailed snakelike on the carpet. The first loop went over her upper chest, just beneath her collarbones. He fiddled at her back, between her shoulder blades, then created another loop over the top rise of her breasts. Again he fiddled, knotting and weaving next to her spinal column.

He was silent. So was she. The sounds and feel of his breath warmed her skin.

Another loop of rope went over her breasts, just below her nipples. He gently eased her flesh so her breasts were trapped in the center of the two binds. The result was, when he'd tightened it, that her nipples were engorged and her breasts appeared swollen in their confines.

He stood before her, studied his work, adjusted the rope slightly, then wrapped more around the base of her ribs.

She stood very still, fingers locked and watching his reflection as he busied around her. He had a look of absolute concentration and occasionally swept his tongue over his bottom lip. There was a bulge in his suit trousers, his erection an outline against the material.

On and on he continued, taking in her wrists now and trapping them in the string of knots she could feel nudging her vertebrae. Her nipples tingled, her breasts reddened. She tried to shift her shoulders, but couldn't.

"Are you okay?"

"Yes, Sir."

He paused and stroked his thumb over her mouth. He then smiled and kissed her. The kiss lingered until he caught her bottom lip between his teeth. He tugged, stretching her skin.

She caught her breath and stared into his eyes.

Excitement danced there, as did lust.

He released her lip and went back to carefully binding her waist and over the curve of her hips.

Imogen's lip stung—she could still feel him there. Her breasts were aching in a low humming sensation, and her pussy was becoming damper, her folds swelling.

He dropped to his knees behind her and ran his hands over the ropes, his fingers weaving in and around them. "Perfect," he murmured. "It's perfect."

Imogen tensed her arms against the knots. She was well and truly trussed up.

He stood, moved in front of her and pressed his hands over her full breasts. "How does it feel?"

She thought for a moment. "Constricting."

"Is it too tight anywhere?"

"No."

"You must tell me." He frowned.

"No, it's fine. I just know I can't move. If I fell, I wouldn't be able to stop myself."

"I'd catch you." He drifted his hands over the ropes, up to her face. "But you won't fall. I won't let you. You're my responsibility and all I can and will think about. If you were hurt I wouldn't forgive myself."

Imogen relaxed her shoulders within the rope.

He must have seen what she'd done. "That's it, breathe normally. It's all fine."

She let her arms relax rather than holding them tense.

"That's it, good girl." He paused. "It feels sexy, doesn't it?"

"I think so, Sir."

He raised his eyebrows and slipped one hand between

her legs, fingering her pussy. "Ah, you're wet and hot, you know damn well it's sexy to be in my ropes, don't try to deny it."

Imogen rocked her hips, wanting more of his touch.

"Tell me it's sexy," he said, rubbing her clit.

"Ah… oh, yes… sexy, it's sexy." Damn, she was so aroused, more than she'd realized, and him doing that…

"Sir," he said a little sharply.

"Sir, it's sexy, Sir."

He gave a lopsided smile and eased a finger high into her entrance.

Imogen felt her knees slacken.

"There we go," he said, pulling out. "That's why we have the bench." He scooped her close and steered her to the middle of the room.

As she walked, her breasts stayed taut and swollen; the rope didn't move, it kept her bound.

Kane maneuvered her to the end of the bench then pressed the center of her back. "Bend over double," he said. "But tell me if it's too uncomfortable on your chest."

She did as he'd asked. The leather was cool on her hot nipples, and as she put her weight lower the sensation in her breasts increased, making them more sensitive and adding to the maelstrom of arousal darting around her body. "It's okay, Sir."

"Good. Now twist your head so you can see me in the mirror."

Again she obeyed.

He was standing directly behind her, still in just his suit trousers. He'd removed his shoes and socks, she wasn't sure when. He looked so big and powerful, so dark and edgy and full of energy.

A tremor of anxiety went through her.

"Shh…" He smoothed his palm over her naked buttocks. "If you need to stop, you know what to say."

"Yes, Sir." She widened her stance. She could do this. She wanted to do this.

"Good." He slipped his fingers down the cleft between her buttocks. He paused at her anus and pressed very gently. "But don't forget *that* word. It's important."

"Yes, Sir." She forced herself not to clench her ass. No one had ever touched or played with her most intimate hole. She had no doubts in her mind Kane would, though. He'd said he had plans for her sweet ass, and she suspected that his plans were about to come to fruition.

A sudden hard slap landed on her right buttock.

She jerked as the flash of pain shot over her skin. She shut her eyes and gasped.

"Watch me," he snapped.

She stared in the mirror again as the burning pain dulled to warm heat.

He was stroking her ass as though admiring the emerging handprint.

"Stunning," he murmured. "Simply stunning."

He raised his hand high.

She knew what was coming and braced.

Another hard whack hit down. Opposite buttock.

Her flesh wobbled as the impact took hold. Her breasts scraped on the bench. She curled her toes and screwed up her face. It had been a solid hit backed up with damn fine male muscle.

"That's it for now," he said, "you took a lot last night." He stooped and kissed her smarting flesh.

His lips were cool against the burn and the adoration in his caresses blissful.

"Mmm..." she said, the now familiar rush of pain stimulating her cunt as she unfurled her toes. "Yes."

His touch left her.

She opened her eyes.

He was fiddling with his belt buckle. He released it then undid his fly. He pushed his trousers down his legs along with his boxer briefs and kicked them aside. His erection stood thick and proud, jutting upward; the head was already filmy with pre-cum. His hair-coated thighs were wide and tense, the curvature of the muscles evident.

Wrapping his fist around the shaft of his cock, he walked to the head end of the bench.

"Open," he instructed, slotting his fingers into her hair and using it to lift her head.

Imogen's scalp stung, sending waves of sweet pain down her spine. She stretched her mouth wide.

He slipped his cock in deep, right to the base of her tongue.

She held her breath and stared at the hair that fanned from his navel to his groin.

He released a soft moan, pulled out, then smoothed back in.

Salty moisture coated her tongue and her cheeks bulged.

He stepped away and rested her head down.

She missed his cock in her mouth. She missed him standing in front of her.

Her knees shook; a drip of moisture eased from her pussy lips to her inner thigh.

"Now you must relax," he said, walking to the bag. "Because it's time."

"For what, Sir?" She hoped it was time for him to fuck her, because damn, that was what her body was screaming out for.

"It is time for this." He held up a small black conical object with a bar at the base. "It's time for me to start preparing your ass for my cock."

She gulped. He was going to fuck her virgin ass?

"Don't worry." He picked up a tube of lube and coated the end of the plug and the tips of the fingers on his right hand. "It will take some time; we'll start off small tonight, but by the time you're ready, in a few weeks you'll be begging for it."

"Yes, Sir." *Begging for it?*

He moved behind her again.

She stared at his reflection and at the plug. That was going inside her? There?

He rubbed his left hand over her ass cheeks, stroking and smoothing her skin. He then transferred the plug to that hand and his lubed fingers stroked over her anus once more.

Imogen gasped and clenched her fists. She could say the safe word if she wanted to, she knew she could. But something in her wanted to find out what the plug would be like. At the club, Tara had apparently loved it. It had heightened her experience from what Imogen could tell.

Kane pressed at the midpoint of her pucker. "Let me in," he whispered.

Imogen forced herself to relax but then tensed as his cool, lubed finger slid into her ass.

"So giving," he said, "you're so perfect and giving. Keep going, just like that."

"Yes, Sir." She kept her concentration on his reflection.

His concentration was on her ass, his elbow bent at just the right angle to get his finger deep, deep, and deeper still.

She tensed her belly, the feeling of invasion so unique. Not unpleasant, just erotically different.

He added another finger.

Her sphincter tightened and a stitch of discomfort ran around the rim. The trickle of moisture from her pussy ran farther down her inner thigh.

He pushed higher, the lube easing the way.

"One day I'll fuck you here," he said. "I'll put my big cock in your ass, balls deep. You'll love it, Imogen, you'll come so hard. I'll have a vibrator in your pussy, too, and your arms and legs bound. It will be amazing, you'll orgasm over and over until you can take no more."

Imogen whimpered, the filthy promise almost too much to think about.

He pulled out and her hole clasped shut. But not for long because then the hard, cool point of the butt plug was there.

"This is no more than my fingers," he said, pressing his left hand against her trapped wrists and holding them over the rope. "Just relax and I'll make it so damn good for you."

She blinked—moisture had collected in the corner of her

eyes. She wanted this, she did, but it was so much. *Kane* was so much. He was pushing her, taking her to new places she never thought she'd visit.

The plug was eased into her body, stretching and filling, Kane drove it on and on.

She gasped, then held her breath. Studied his naked form and his heavy erection and the sight of herself, ass up, being invaded back there.

"That's it, nearly in…" he said.

Imogen didn't think she could take any more. The flare of the base was so much, too much. It hurt, it nipped… "Oww…"

"You've done it," he said.

A sudden easing of her sphincter told her the plug was fully inserted. She tensed her pelvic muscles. She felt full, dense, the plug pressing on nerves that seemed to be attached to her pussy.

She groaned and closed her eyes. She wanted to come, she wanted release.

"Hey." Kane was in front of her. He kissed the tip of her nose. "Do you need to say anything?"

She opened her eyes. He was frowning and he looked worried.

"Say it if you need to," he said. "I don't want to push you too far."

"I do… need to say… something."

A fleeting glimpse of sadness crossed his face. "Say it," he whispered.

She swallowed and sucked in a deep breath. "Fuck me. Fuck me now… Sir."

He tilted his chin, his lips tightened. He nodded. "With pleasure."

In three fast paces he was behind her. He gripped her hips, lined up his cock with her pussy, and forged in.

Imogen was bumped up the table. His balls crushed up to her labia and her clit rubbed against the leather.

She cried out in pleasure and shock. With her ass already

full, distended, his cock felt bigger than ever inside her.

"You like that?" he asked, withdrawing, then thrusting back in.

"Yes... yes, Sir..."

She set her blurry focus on their reflection in the mirror. They looked animalistic, primal. Fucking, bound, grunting and groaning.

Kane's lips were pulled back, his teeth bared. He held her tight, his belly slamming onto the base of the butt plug on each ride to full depth.

Imogen surrendered to it all. A climax was racing her way but she had no control over it. Kane would wring it out of her.

She panted and struggled to catch her breath. The orgasm had arrived. Her legs shook, her breasts dragged on the bench, and the collar dug into her neck as she strained against all her binds. She'd never felt so wild and free, yet she couldn't move at all.

"Come, come, sub..." he shouted, delivering a sudden hard slap to her right buttock.

Imogen tipped over the edge. The pressure that had built within her burst free, dragging her with it on a rollercoaster of ecstasy. Her skin was on fire, her limbs trembled, and her pussy overflowed with bliss.

"Yes, oh God, yes, squeeze me with your cunt like that..." Kane tilted his head to the ceiling; his chest heaved and his abdominal muscles turned to a stack of bricks.

As he emptied his pleasure into her, Imogen was in awe of his beauty. He was the epitome of a man, not afraid to admit to his needs and take what he wanted.

A sob burst up from her as another orgasmic spasm ravaged her pussy and her clit rammed solidly on the bench.

He withdrew, shoved back in, his cock coated in juice and cum.

"Oh, my God..." he said. "I'm not usually a man to pray..." He gave another slower ride in and out. "But thank you, God, for delivering Imogen to me."

Imogen gasped for breath. The ropes were tight now that she was so breathless. "Kane... I..." She couldn't finish.

He withdrew and lifted her upright. She dragged in air. Her breasts felt like they might burst, so did her lungs.

"Are you okay?" He ran his hands down her back, his fingers tapping over the knots.

She was too breathless to speak. Suddenly the ropes loosened around her chest. Her lungs expanded fully and her breasts were freed.

Kane stepped behind her, the rope slackened more, and within another few seconds were in a heap at her feet.

"Talk to me," he said, holding her by the shoulders. "Are you okay?"

"Yes..." She pressed a hand over her aching chest. "Yes..."

"Sure?"

"Yes, it was just so..." God, the plug, it was still there. "So much, and tipped over and bound it felt like I couldn't catch my breath."

"But you could." He hugged her close. "And you can now."

"I know." She slipped her hands around his waist and rested her cheek over the three stars.

He kissed the top of her head. "That was amazing. You're amazing, we're so good together."

His softening cock pressed on her belly. "Yes. I think so too." She paused. "The plug...?"

"I want you to keep it in. I want you to use it, most days for a while, and then, soon, you'll be ready for me to claim that final bit of you to make you mine."

# CHAPTER SEVENTEEN

Kane helped Imogen into the bed and after tucking the sheets around her, he went to the window and flung open the black curtains.

From this room, the Empire State Building stole the view and was still illuminated bright red.

"I thought you might like to go to sleep looking at that," he said.

"Yes," Imogen murmured, her body heavy and weary.

He slid in beside her, spooning her so they could both look at the skyline.

He was so warm and solid, his embrace so comforting. Imogen couldn't remember ever feeling so content. They weren't just a fling or a casual couple, they were going to give it a go, as a relationship. They'd decided that, together. The last thing she saw as she shut her eyes was the tip of the building that glowed red, just for her.

A drifting sensation came over her, and her thoughts mellowed and softened, as did her breathing. Somewhere between sleep and awake she was vaguely aware of Kane kissing her, just behind her ear.

"I love you," he whispered.

Imogen was too lost in the world of slumber to reply and

wasn't even sure if it was real. Dreams were sneaking up on her, a floating sensation carrying her into the night. She let herself fall, surrendered to exhaustion and blissed-out contentment.

Kane loved her?

• • • • • • •

She woke; it was sometime later, she knew that because there was a faint lilac glow behind the Empire State Building, signifying dawn.

Kane was still wrapped around her, his breathing steady and deep and his chest pressing against her back. She shifted slightly and became aware of the plug.

Carefully, she slipped from Kane's embrace. He mumbled and turned but didn't wake. She stood and tiptoed back to her room, needing to use the bathroom.

Once inside, she removed the plug, washed it in hot soapy water, and placed it in a spare cosmetic bag. She felt tender, not just her ass but her pussy and her breasts too. She used the toilet, then splashed water on her face. Brushed her teeth, and set about removing the pins from her hair.

She had a glow to her cheeks and her eyes sparkled the way Kane's had during their scene the evening before. Was that what love looked like? Was that what she looked like in love? It had been so long, she'd only told one man before that she loved him and he'd left her—it hadn't been a confession she'd been in a hurry to make again.

But Kane... did she love him? Yes. She knew she did. And she could still hear him quietly saying those words in her ear. It hadn't been a dream, she was sure of it now.

Once her hair was loose and flowing around her shoulders, she ran her fingers over the collar. It was still an alien concept to wear it all the time—what would her colleagues say? They'd think she'd agreed to become someone's pet. But of course, she knew what it meant, what it signified. She decided to leave it on. Perhaps when they woke naked and warm and sleepy, they'd make love again and she'd call him Sir so that he got that dreamy look on his face as she fulfilled his fantasy.

Smiling, she padded naked back to bed. She carefully slotted herself next to Kane and wound her arm over his belly, her head resting by his upper arm. "I love you too," she whispered, then kissed the ball of his shoulder.

• • • • • • •

When she woke the bed was empty, but she could hear Kane's deep voice and guessed he was on the phone.

She turned and faced the window. The red lights had gone from the Empire State Building and the sun shone bright from a clear blue sky.

Kane was dressed in a suit and tie, his mobile pressed to his ear, and he was pacing backward and forward from one side of the window to the other.

"Yes, I know, it's hardly ideal." Pause. "Well, what did Ryland say?" Pause. "I can't believe this, it was as good as in the bag. It's a total fuck-up." He shoved his hand through his hair, stopped and stared at the floor.

Imogen propped herself onto her elbow. He didn't sound happy at all.

"Well, I understand that, it's just damn inconvenient, it's hardly around the corner, is it?" He sighed. "But I suppose I have no choice, not if he's insisting on seeing me before signing. It's too important to not be there." He looked at Imogen and frowned. "Yes, I'm still in New York, but I'll be in San Francisco by the end of the day. Set up an evening meeting with him and make sure he brings his lawyer because I'll have mine." He clicked his phone shut and jabbed it into his inner jacket pocket.

"Problems?" Imogen said.

*He's going to San Francisco?*

"No more than usual." He shook his head and tutted. "This company has put up barriers every step of the way to merging with one of my communication enterprises, but at the end of the day I'm saving them from bankruptcy. I don't know why they're being so stubborn or so demanding."

"That's kind of you, to help them out."

"Not kind, it's in my best interest to have their assets. Kind doesn't come into the business world." He walked over to the bed and dropped a kiss on her cheek. "How are you?"

"Fine." She smiled up at him. He smelled heavenly. "You?"

"Very well." He straightened. "I've called for breakfast, but before it arrives, get up and dressed, we have to go soon."

"Go where?"

"To the airport. We'll be flying to San Francisco in a few hours." He reached for his phone again. Whoever he called answered immediately. "Jenson, it's me, we're heading to the West Coast, San Fran, as soon as possible. Text me the takeoff slot." He looked at Imogen. "Two passengers." He ended the call and again shoved the phone away.

"I can't go to San Francisco," she said.

"Yes, you can."

"No, I can't. I thought the plan was for us to fly back to London tomorrow, I'm due back at work the day after."

"So take the day off." He shoved his hands into his trouser pockets and shrugged. "In fact, take the week off."

Imogen stared at him. He didn't seem in the least bit concerned about her concerns. "I can't take the week off," she said. "I have meetings and conference calls and deadlines that must be met by this Friday. I also have some quarterly reviews to get done for my team, it's important."

"We can fix that. Bob Thornton is still on the board at Coutts, isn't he?"

"Well, yes, but…"

"We've done business before. I'll call him, explain that you won't be in this week, that you're with me."

"You can't do that." She stared at him wide-eyed. "You

can't."

"Of course I can." He pulled his phone out again.

"No!"

"What's the problem?" He frowned and appeared to notice her agitation for the first time.

"What's the problem?" She sat on the edge of the bed, allowing the sheet to slip from around her bare body. "The problem is it's my job. I have to be there, they can't just put someone else in in my place, I'm not that replaceable, or at least I hope not."

"I'm sure it will be very difficult to replace you, but the bottom line is you don't have to do anything about it. I'll personally offer to cover the cost of an agency worker to fill your shoes this week so you don't have a ton of work to cope with if you eventually want go back to the office."

"What...?" She stood. "Bloody hell, Kane. You can't do that, and of course it's what I want to do."

"We'll talk about that later." He smiled and touched her cheek with the back of his thumb. "And this week is not a problem. What's the point in having money if I can't use it to get what I want... and I want you. I want you with me in San Francisco."

Imogen opened her mouth but no words came out. He thought she was pissed about him spending money on her replacement, when in fact, she was furious that he thought he could tell her what to do and thought she might not go back to her office.

"One phone call," he said, scrolling through his contacts. "That's all it will take."

"No." She grabbed the phone from him and held it aloft.

"What the"—he gave her a steely look—"hell are you doing?"

"If you call Bob Thornton, I swear I'll walk out of here and you'll never see me again."

"Imogen." He scowled. "Remember who you are speaking to and also remember to address me as Sir." He retrieved his phone and set it on the table that still held the long black ropes and the squat brown bag.

"Sir? Sir? No, I'm not addressing you as bloody Sir, we're having a conversation about me getting back to work."

He rubbed his hand over his temple as if he was weary and stared at her. "There is no conversation to be had. You're coming with me to the West Coast and I will let your superiors know." He sighed, stepped close, and placed his hands on her shoulders. "Now don't concern yourself with this another minute. I'll have it taken care of by the time you're out of the shower. There is nothing for you to worry about." He rubbed his finger over the collar she still wore. "Now go and get ready like I told you to."

"You can't tell me... to do... anything..." She was still wearing the collar and as she'd spoken, she realized why he was being the way he was.

"You keep forgetting to address me as Sir." He frowned. "And speaking to me like this will get you a spanking."

Imogen stepped away from him. She reached behind her neck and undid the tiny buckle. The collar was the reason why he was speaking to her this way and insisting she do as she was told without question. It was because he was seeing her as his submissive, yet she wasn't, not now, not when they were discussing matters that were so important to her—which her career most certainly was.

She slid the collar from her neck and held it out to him. "Here, this is yours."

He didn't take it. "No, it's yours and I want you to wear it."

"We discussed this already. I said I'd wear it when we were, when you are..."

"In the bedroom was one of the words you used."

"Yes."

"And we're in a bedroom now." He pointed at the bed.

"Don't twist it, you know what I meant." Her nakedness suddenly felt acute and uncomfortable. She stepped past him and plucked a black toweling robe from a hook, shrugged into it.

He watched as she tightened the belt around her waist. "Imogen, don't be like this. I want to be with you, I thought you wanted to be with me? We agreed to that last night."

"I do want to be with you." Oh, she did, desperately so. He'd become the gravitational force that all her thoughts and hopes and dreams of the future were spinning around.

"So come with me." His voice softened. "Today. Stay with me."

"I'd love to, but…"

"There are no buts, not if you don't want there to be." He stepped closer and touched the knot she'd just secured at her waist. "I thought we'd decided to give it a go, be a couple. I thought you understood that would mean you giving up work and accompanying me."

"Accompanying you?" How could they have misunderstood each other so drastically? "Give up work?"

"Yes. You know my business takes me around the globe on a continual business trip. Yes, I have apartments in several cities plus a villa in the Caribbean and a yacht in St. Tropez, but I live out of hotels, that's my home."

"That's not a good way to be." She shook her head.

"It's the way it is. I have to keep my finger on the pulse of so many organizations."

"Can't you delegate?"

"I delegate plenty, but some occasions, like today, only my presence will do."

"But… I can't come with you around the globe." She paused as a tightening in her chest warned that a sob and tears could possibly burst free. "I have a home, a job. I have a best friend, my mother, and a life in London. You don't really expect me to give all that up after a few days with you?"

"It's not a few days, it's been a long time coming. We're right for each other." He slid his hand up to her face and cupped her cheek. "And it's time for us to be together, permanently."

Imogen swallowed, her mouth was dry and her throat

thick. She shook her head. "I want you in my life permanently, Kane, but I can't give up mine to live in yours."

"Why not?"

"Because I still have things I want to achieve, I have goals." She rested her hand over his. "I'm self-sufficient, I have been for a long time. I can't just let a man look after me, no matter how many millions you have in the bank."

"It's billions, for the record."

"I know, I see your balance, remember… It's who I am, your bank manager."

"But I want you to be so much more. I want you to be at my side."

"No." She looked away. She couldn't stand to see the pain in his eyes. "I need to go back to London, back to my life, and if you're there, in London, then I'd love to see you."

"I won't be in London for months."

"Then I won't see you for months."

"Imogen." He snatched her close, his mouth almost touching hers.

She gasped and pressed her hands over his suit jacket.

"Don't talk crazy," he said, his voice low and dense with emotion. "Not after all we've done…"

"It's not crazy." Tears were forming now, the happiness she thought was hers fluttering away like petals in the wind. "I've worked too hard to throw my career down the drain, and you seem to think I will in the blink of an eye." As she'd said the word 'blink,' a tear spilled over and rolled down her cheek.

He caught it with his thumb and smeared it away.

"I'm sorry," she said, "that I misunderstood when you said you wanted us to be a couple. I had no idea that would mean giving up such a huge part of who I am."

Still he didn't speak. He just stared at her, confusion in his eyes and also pain.

"Kane…"

"Just when I thought I had it all," he said quietly.

"Me too."

He dragged down the corners of his mouth. "Most women would happily give it all up and be taken care of by a rich man who adores them."

"I'm not most women, as has been previously pointed out."

"Don't I know it." He squeezed his eyes shut. "A fact that has well and truly bitten me on the ass right now."

"I'm sorry." She pulled away and turned to the window, wrapped her arms around herself—not being in his arms made her cold.

"So you won't come to San Francisco today?"

"No. I have to go back to the UK as planned and work this week."

"And I can't say anything to persuade you to change your mind?"

She stared at an airplane making a frothy trail in the sky. "About this week or giving up my career?"

"Both."

"No, I don't think so. I…" She turned to him. She wanted to say she loved him, that he meant the world to her. But would that declaration change anything? He was as stubborn as she, and when they both saw their futures so differently there was no middle ground.

"What?" he said.

"I… nothing." She shook her head and stared at her red toenails. "Nothing at all."

"I'm not saying goodbye to you," he said.

"Then I'll say it for you."

"No…"

"If you expect me to give everything up for you, it has to be goodbye, Kane." She looked up at him. "Thank you for a wonderful trip and for… enlightening me. But I guess this is as far as we go."

He tilted his chin and narrowed his eyes.

She turned to the window again. She couldn't stand to see what she was putting him through with her decision and her words.

Outside, New York carried on as it had yesterday, but for her, everything had changed. She couldn't give the man she loved what he wanted.

It was too much.

He was asking for more than she could give.

The door slammed and she spun around. The room was empty. He'd left.

"Oh, fuck," she said, feeling her limbs tremble and her belly clench. "Fuck, fuck, fuck…" The tears she'd been holding back rushed to be free, rolling in big, fat drips down her cheeks.

It was over? It had only just started. She felt like she'd been put on a rollercoaster ride of bliss the last few days and it had all suddenly crashed down around her. She was left hanging, bruised and battered and dangling in space.

She stared at the door. Should she go after him? Tell him she would do as he'd asked. Throw everything away that she'd worked for to be his constant companion—his submissive?

Her feet stayed firmly planted where she was. She couldn't do it. A few whirlwind days and some of the finest sex of her life couldn't persuade her to abandon her position or shelve her ambitions.

# CHAPTER EIGHTEEN

Imogen had flown back to London first class on a ticket Kane's secretary arranged to have waiting at the departure desk.

She'd sat with an eye mask on—it wasn't a night flight, but her eyes were red and swollen from crying as she'd packed then made her way to JFK. They were quiet tears of regret and also disappointment. How quickly the pendulum of life had swung from delight to despair.

"What the bloody hell has he done to you?" Clarris exclaimed when Imogen turned up at her door that evening.

"Nothing."

"Doesn't look like nothing." Clarris ushered her in. "There's wine in the fridge, grab it. I'll just put Katie's latest Disney obsession on."

Imogen ruffled Katie's fine blond hair and smiled. "Hi, Katie."

"Imo, Imo," she said, "you back."

"Yes, I'm back. I got you this." She held out the tiny t-shirt and little teddy she'd picked up from the Fifth Avenue gift shop.

"Thank you," Katie said, grabbing them, then dashing off as the sound of the movie came from the living area.

"Now," Clarris said, reappearing. "Tell me all about it."

She gathered the wine and two glasses and settled on the sofa, legs tucked beneath her.

"There's not much to tell." Imogen flopped down next to her, her limbs exhausted.

"You turn up here looking like you've sobbed all the way across the Atlantic and there's not much to tell. Pull the other one, darling."

Imogen swallowed and looked away.

"Fuck, you did cry all the way across the Atlantic, didn't you?"

"Not all the way, I—"

"Bastard. I always knew there was something dubious about Kane Ward. Too damn squeaky clean. Everyone has dirt, no one is that pure."

"He didn't do anything, not really." As Imogen spoke, she pictured him in her mind's eye. His face when she'd said goodbye, how he'd refused to say it. She was hurting but she'd hurt him too, and that was almost as painful.

"So what happened?"

"It was amazing, we had a lovely time."

"Until?" Clarris passed her a glass of white wine.

"He…" She paused. "He was sweet—"

"Kane Ward sweet, that's not the first adjective I'd use for him." Clarris made a scoffing sound.

"Well, he was, and romantic and caring. He took me to dinner, bought me flowers, we went to the top of the Empire State Building at night…"

"Yeah, well. I'll give him that then." She shrugged. "That sounds pretty romantic."

Imogen decided not to mention the extravagant display of flowers or the fact one of the tallest buildings in Manhattan had been lit red to show his adoration of her. That did seem a bit much now, especially how the conversation they'd had up there had been so misinterpreted by each of them.

"And what else?" Clarris knocked back some wine. "He

seduced you, obviously."

"Yes." Imogen glanced away as memories of the club, the cross, the rope, and the plug flashed through her mind.

"What? Tell me."

Sometimes, having an investigative journalist as a best friend could be wearing. Imogen didn't want to divulge everything, but she needed to talk to someone or she'd go round the bend.

"Did he have a really small dick? Premature ejaculation," Clarris asked. "No, no, wait, I bet he's kinky, got a penchant for taking it where the sun doesn't shine with a big black strap-on, or—"

"No," Imogen said, looking Clarris in the eye. "He did not want to do anything like that." She hoped she'd put enough conviction into her words, because Clarris could sniff out a lie a mile away. "And for the record, the sex was great, he's anatomically perfect, and no instances of reaching the finish line too early."

"Good to hear it." Clarris sighed. "Damn, if only I could have a grade A shag I'd feel so much better."

"Maybe that's what it is," Imogen said, resting back. "I had it and now it's gone again, the gap that I'd filled with other things is gaping again and I've remembered what I'm missing."

"But why has it gone?" Clarris rested her hand on Imogen's arm. "What happened? It's just between us, I promise. I'd never say or do anything to hurt you, you know I wouldn't."

"I know that." Imogen put her hand over her friend's. "And it's nothing dramatic really. He actually didn't do anything wrong, it's just a case of wanting to be together but not being able to be."

"Why not?"

"He spends his time roaming the globe checking on his empire. His constant traveling is hardly conducive to a relationship."

"So can't you just go with him? I bet he stays in all the

best hotels."

"Yes, he does." She thought of the fabulous suite she'd enjoyed the last few days. "And he has apartments, villas, and yachts."

"And a private jet to get him around." Clarris shrugged and looked at Imogen over the rim of her wine glass. "Doesn't sound like a bad option to me."

"But I have a job, a life, you and Katie, and what about Mum?"

"Of course you do, and that's wonderful, but… for God's sake, this is Kane Ward. You'd never have to work or wash up, or clean your own clothes again. Life would be all champagne and caviar and glamorous locations."

"It would be." Imogen glanced at Katie. She was engrossed in her movie, thumb in her mouth and hugging the new teddy. Maybe one day she and Kane would have had a child. She wouldn't have had to worry about maternity leave and childcare the way Clarris had to. She wouldn't have had any of the worries of ordinary people ever again.

She found herself stroking her neck, thinking of the collar. How he'd ordered her to get dressed and get ready to go with him. He'd spoken with such authority, he'd presumed she'd obey—he was used to being obeyed by a sub in a collar.

"You got a sore throat?" Clarris asked. "I always get something after I've been long haul."

"No, it's fine. I just…"

"You're just wondering if you've thrown away the best thing that ever happened to you."

"No, not at all." Imogen drained the last of her wine and stood. "He was asking too much. I couldn't give it."

"Well, I admire your determination to be an independent woman," Clarris said. "You off already?"

"Yes, I'm knackered. A glass of wine and now I just need bed. Thanks, though…"

"That's what friends are for. I'm here if you need me."

• • • • • •

Imogen tossed and turned that night. Despite her being exhausted, sleep was hard to find. When she did she dreamed of Kane. He was beside her, his hand pressing on the small of her back and urging her forward. She could see the roses, the scarlet Empire State Building, the piano with a single red rose reflected in its surface. Then she was in his arms, smiling up at him, her fingers smoothing over the stars on his chest as his lips brushed hers. She was bound to the cross with ropes around her chest and squeezing her breasts. She wanted more, more of everything. His hands on her ass, his fingers in her pussy, his mouth on her nipples. She was panting for it, her heart racing. An orgasm was there, over-spilling, dragging her pelvic muscles into blissful spasms.

She woke sweating and her pussy thumping through the final stages of a swift climax.

"Kane," she gasped, spreading her legs and arms over to the empty side of the bed.

Suddenly tears came again. But not the slow, silent ones that dripped heavily down her cheeks on the plane. These were fast and furious, sharp and harsh, they stung her eyes and soaked the pillow. The accompanying sobs were painful; they racked her chest and burned her throat.

When had she become such a crybaby? She thumped the pillow, frustrated with herself. But that didn't stop the tears. On and on they came until she slumped, exhausted, her hand at her neck, wishing she could go back to the night before and have Kane spooned around her, making her feel safe and adored.

The sound of the alarm dragged her from a deep and mercifully dreamless sleep. As she lifted her head she felt the dried moisture from her nighttime sobbing scratch her cheek. A strand of hair was crusted to her lip.

Well, that was it, done. She wasn't going to cry over Kane Ward anymore. She'd put it all down to experience and get on with her life. One weepy trip across an ocean and a pitiful bout of pillow sobbing was enough to spend on any man, billionaire or not.

She jumped into the shower, humming *I'm going to wash that man right out of my hair*, then dried and wandered to her wardrobe in search of her favorite black skirt suit.

As she walked past the mirror she paused. Her fractionally brighter mood slipped away. There was a mark on her hip. She spun to check out the crimson trail then traced it with her fingertip. It wasn't sore, but there was a definite line left from the rope Kane had bound her with.

She backed up, wanting a closer inspection. On her ass cheeks were tiny purple-red dots, like a rash of minuscule bruises.

From the paddle.

She felt her eyes tingle. He'd certainly left his mark on her both emotionally and physically.

"Stop it." She moved from the mirror. "Enough." She pulled on underwear, then her clothes for the office. Out of sight, out of mind. She just wouldn't look at her ass until she was sure the evidence of Kane was gone.

But would she miss the marks? They were a reminder of what they'd done, and damn it, it had been so good. She'd gone to new highs, had experienced intense, mind-blowing orgasms that had left her breathless and nearly unconscious. How would she feel going back to vanilla sex? If she had a one-night stand and it was straight, no excitement, no added stimuli...

Who was she kidding? She had no desire at the moment to allow anyone but Kane into her bed. There wouldn't be any one-night stands, not for a long time. And then... well, then she'd just have to see if he'd ruined her for all other men.

She poured tea, made toast but had no appetite, so headed into the office. She was greeted with a pile of paperwork and long to-do list, but it was for the best. Work would keep Kane Ward off her mind—as long as she didn't have to handle any of his accounts, that was.

• • • • • •

But she did. Over the next month there were several big transactions on Kane Ward's account that she couldn't help but notice. He'd acquired a large plot of land in Kent, a ten-million-pound townhouse in Kensington, and sold a villa in Spain. He'd also bought a Bentley and his jet had required a new engine that was the price of the average house before any charges had been made for fitting it. He'd thrown money at The Shard too, purchasing floor space.

Every time she saw his name her heart ached. It was a real physical tugging in her chest that didn't get easier as the weeks went on. She'd immersed herself in work, staying until late every evening. She'd hung out with Clarris and Katie at weekends—when they'd been there, but Katie was busy with Tumbletots and play dates now she was getting older.

August came around, and as was typical, the rain arrived too. Clarris always called it London's rainy season and Imogen thought she'd probably got it right. She stared at the dishwater-gray sky and the streaks of rain on her office window.

*Is this what life is all about? Just a treadmill of work and lonely nights?*

She wondered where in the world Kane was. Somewhere hot and tropical? Perhaps near a beach—if so, no doubt a private one with waiter service and a yacht moored just beyond the breaking waves.

She wondered who he was with. It hurt to think about that, but her brain didn't seem to have any consideration for her heart. Was he with a beautiful, naked submissive? Was she wearing his collar? The one Imogen had worn? Or perhaps he was at a club with a posy of willing women all at his feet, begging him to take the flogger to their rears and fuck them till they couldn't breathe.

She shuddered and beat down a wave of nausea. She'd never been a jealous sort, but the thought of Kane making another woman feel how he'd made her feel was enough to create a buildup of bile in her gullet.

The rain was a depressing view, so she turned back to her desk and picked up her pen. Her mobile phone rang. It wasn't a number she recognized.

"Hello," she said.

"Imogen, is that you?" A female with an American accent.

"Yes. Who is this?"

"It's Marie, we met in New York in June." She paused. "I was with Taylor Ward."

"Oh, oh yes, of course, I'm sorry, how are you?"

"I'm fine, and you?"

"Yes, very good." That wasn't the truth but it was the polite answer, and why was Marie calling her? "How is the new business coming along?"

"Very well, I've got my first designs coming off the desk and into reality and two shows set up for Fashion Week."

"Wow, that sounds great, congratulations."

"Thanks." Marie paused. "Kane was here this weekend, in New York."

"Oh, was he?" Well, at least now she knew he wasn't on a beach with a bunch of semi-clad submissive beauties.

"Yes. He and Taylor talked until late into the night."

"At the club?"

"No. He didn't want to go to the club. We went to the same restaurant we all went to last time. Sat at the same table, your seat obviously empty, and then he wanted to come back to the apartment and talk to his brother."

"Oh," Imogen said again. "I see." What did this have to do with her? She didn't know but she was glad of the information on the man who was still very much in control of her heart. He was okay, that was good, and if he was spending time with his brother that was a positive thing. Family was important.

"It was strange," Marie went on. "You not being there. You seemed so... connected, you and Kane."

"Yes, we were."

"So what went wrong?"

"Well, I..." She didn't know if she really wanted to go into details. She and Marie were hardly best buddies.

"I'm sorry, I shouldn't be so forthright, but you know us Americans, we just say it how it is, not like you British with the stiff upper lip thing. Trouble is, Imogen, that man is really damn miserable and the only thing that Taylor says has changed is you've disappeared from his life."

"Yes, I have disappeared. That pretty much sums it up." She rubbed her fingers over the bridge of her nose and squeezed. She wouldn't cry, not here. Not at work.

"Was it the BDSM, the club?"

"No, actually it wasn't anything to do with that." Imogen glanced at her office door, double-checking it was properly shut. "That was new for me, yes, but also exciting, and let's face it, I was in the hands of an expert."

"That's true."

"So it was all pretty damn good in that department."

"I can believe it."

"It's just... his nomadic lifestyle. How can that be compatible with a relationship?"

"Nomadic?"

"I'll admit it's a very luxurious way to live, but I have a job in London and friends, family not too far away that depend on me. I want to spend time with them."

"Of course you do."

"And I can't just throw away my career."

"No, I understand that perfectly."

"And he expected me to just walk away from it all."

Marie was quiet.

"How did you get my number?" Imogen asked.

"Taylor took it from Kane's phone when he stepped out the room. He gave it to me and told me to call you, make sure you were okay."

"That's kind of you."

"And are you okay? The truth this time."

"No, I miss him, but I don't see a way around the problem."

"There is always a way around problems if you want there to be. Maybe you just need to meet in the middle."

"I'm happy for that, but he has no middle ground. Kane is a man who is used to getting what he wants. When he didn't this time he threw his very expensive toys from the pram and walked away."

"I see." She sighed. "Listen, I have to go. But Taylor and I just wanted you to know that Kane misses you, he regrets how it ended, and if you're feeling bad, he's feeling worse."

"I doubt it."

"Take care, Imogen," she said. "And I'm sorry, I thought we'd be spending more time together. I was looking forward to having you as my friend."

"I feel the same. Thanks for calling."

Marie hung up.

Imogen placed her phone down. Her head spun. She felt like she'd just been dropped into Kane's world again. She tried not to feel jealous that Marie and Taylor had gone to dinner with him; she would have loved to have been there.

She rested her head in her hands and stared at a complex transaction she needed to check through. She sighed. Yes, she loved her job, the fact she was breaking through the glass ceiling at Coutts, but was it worth her heart being torn in two?

Maybe she was being as stubborn as Kane. She'd complained that he had no middle ground, but perhaps she was equally as guilty of the crime.

She picked up her pen. She had to get this work done. Push Kane and Taylor and Marie from her mind and carry on. Besides, the sooner she did, the sooner she'd be able to knock off work and collect the Chinese takeaway she'd promised Clarris they'd have for supper.

# CHAPTER NINETEEN

"Mmm, smells good," Clarris said, letting Imogen into the apartment.

"Sorry it's a bit late." Imogen stepped past her, holding a bag heavy with hot food.

"No, it's fine, Katie's only just gone down."

"You had a good day?" Imogen asked, putting the takeaway on the kitchen table, then plucking out cartons of noodles, chicken, and stir-fry.

"Busy, busy, got a royal scandal about to unfold so I had to send a few to cover that, which left me short on another thing, and then… anyway, lots of juggling the team around."

"Oh, what's the royal scandal?"

"It will hit the papers in the morning. The usual prince up to the usual shenanigans, but in a pool in Crete this time. Some great pictures have been leaked, we'll have to censor parts of them, they're so explicit. Damn shame, though; he's hot."

Imogen laughed. "That sounds quite a scoop."

"It is."

Clarris' job seemed so far removed from Imogen's and she liked hearing about it.

They filled up plates with food and sat on the sofa for a

TV dinner. Clarris put the news on low volume, as was her habit.

"So how has your day been?" Clarris asked, swirling noodles onto her fork.

"Okay, got plenty done—it's like that when the weather is bad, it makes me get my head down." She paused. "I did get a bit of a strange phone call, though."

"Oh?"

"Yes, Marie, Kane's brother's…" She hesitated. What was she? Girlfriend, fiancée, wife? She was his submissive, his woman, but she couldn't go into that with Clarris, not now.

"What?" Clarris said, cocking her head. "Kane's brother's what?"

"His girlfriend, they're pretty serious." That should cover it. "She called me."

"Really? What did she want?"

"Just to say Kane had been there."

"And…" Clarris spun her fork in the air as if trying to roll the words out of Imogen's mouth. "What else?"

Imogen shrugged. "I think what she was trying to say is that he misses me."

"Good, I hope his heart is shattered into a million little pieces and beyond repair." She huffed.

"Clarris."

"Well, after what he did to you." She scowled.

"He didn't do anything, not really."

"He made you miserable; why or how is irrelevant, the end result is the same. I swear I'll find something on him and splash it all over the front cover of the *Daily News*."

"No, he doesn't deserve that." Imogen paused. "But she got me thinking."

"Why? What else did she say?"

"It was more what I said, really. I told her that he wouldn't meet me halfway and then I wondered if maybe I was guilty of the same. Perhaps we've both been stubborn and all the time I thought it was him being the obstinate one."

"He wanted you to throw everything away for him. That wasn't a halfway demand."

Demand. Yes, that's what it had been. No wonder it had put her hackles up. Time had blurred her memory, but Clarris had remembered the story perfectly.

"Yes, you're right." Imogen sighed. "There wasn't anywhere to meet halfway and—"

*Bang. Bang. Bang.*

The sound of a fist rather than knuckles rapping at the front door echoed around the room.

"You expecting someone?" Imogen asked.

"No." Clarris glanced at Katie's bedroom door. "No one." She stood. "I hope that hasn't woken her up. Bloody inconsiderate this time of evening."

"You want me to go and see who it is?" Imogen placed her plate on the table.

"No, it's fine. I'll go. I'll put the chain on. Probably Bible people again. They've been round twice this month already trying to correct the error of my ways. Keep an eye out in case she wanders out of her room, though."

"Okay." Imogen rested back and glanced at the bedroom, then the TV. The weather was on. Looked like sun for the next few days, thank goodness.

Voices came from the hallway—Clarris no doubt being sarcastic to the unwanted visitors and amusing herself.

"Imogen."

A deep, heart-wrenchingly familiar voice startled Imogen and she turned to the doorway.

Kane stood there. Dressed all in back, stubble thick and his eyes narrowed.

"What… what are you doing here?" she asked, her focus blurring at the shock of seeing him there. It was completely out of context for Kane Ward to be standing in Clarris' lounge.

"I went to your apartment," he said. "You weren't there. I remembered you mentioned your friend lived next door. I took a chance."

Clarris appeared behind him. Her eyes were wide and she gave Imogen an apologetic shrug. "Sorry," she mouthed.

"So here I am," he said, tilting his chin.

"But...?" She sat forward and pushed her hand through her hair. Was she dreaming? Was this really happening?

"And we're going to talk this through," he said. "Now."

God, he looked so damn gorgeous. The Band-Aids she'd applied to her heartache fell away and it hurt all over again that he wasn't hers—that she wasn't his. "Talk what through?"

"Us. Come on."

*Us?* "But I..." What else was there to say? Why was he doing this? It just prolonged the agony.

He walked up to her and reached for her hand, pulling her to standing. "Are those your keys?" he asked, indicating a bunch on the table with a Costa Coffee fob.

"Yes."

He scooped them up, then in one swift move scooped her up too.

"Kane, ahhh... what?"

He'd stooped low and swung her over his shoulder. Imogen's world was suddenly upside down and she was staring at his ass. She went to kick but he'd braced her legs with his arm. She grabbed for his belt to support her upper body as her hair fell forward over her face. "Kane!"

"I'm sorry to interrupt your meal, Clarris," Kane said in a perfectly calm voice, as though he didn't have a woman hoisted over his shoulder. "But there is something I must discuss with Imogen."

"That's all right," Clarris said. "I'll get the door."

Imogen wriggled furiously. Damn it. Clarris wasn't going to save her. "Kane, put me down. What are you, a Neanderthal?"

"No, just a man who will be heard out."

"Bloody hell." She banged his back with her fist as the

carpet turned to hallway flooring.

He opened her front door with her key and went inside. He slammed the door shut with a swift kick.

"Put me down," she said, her cheeks hot and red. "Now."

This time he listened to her. He placed her on the floor with her back to the wall, then flicked on the light.

She stared up at him, her pulse raging in her ears and her belly still tense from being pressed against his shoulder. "What the...?"

He stepped forward and banged his palms on the wall on either side of her head. "I told you I wasn't going to say goodbye, Imogen. It's not in my vocabulary to say that to you."

That was true.

"I knew back then I had to see you again," he added.

"There are other ways of seeing me than hoisting me over your shoulder and... and kidnapping me."

He gave a sly smile. "Part of my plan. Minimal risk of not getting you where I want you."

"And have you got me where you want me?" Her heart was going to explode, she was sure of it. She was mad at him, she wanted to fling her arms around him. She wanted to slap his face, then kiss him all over.

"Yes," he said, leaning closer. "I have. Now all you need to do is listen."

She stared at his lips as he spoke. A mouth she knew so well and had missed so much. Was he going to kiss her? She ached for that, needed it so badly. But what good would come of it? It would only show her what she was missing.

"You can do that, can't you?" he asked.

"What?"

"Listen."

She nodded. "Yes," she said quietly. "I can listen."

"Good, come on." He took her hand.

"But what's all this about?" Imogen asked as he led her into her living area.

"I told you. Us."

"There is no us." She untangled her hand from his and folded her arms, stood in the center of the room. "It can't work."

"There is no such thing as can't, and I beg to differ, there is an us, Imogen, very much so."

She pressed her lips together. She didn't want to argue with that. Being an *us* with Kane Ward was something she longed to be again. "Okay." She nodded. "I'm listening."

"Good." He looked around her home. Soft seating covered in bright cushions sat before a tall bookcase that could be tidier. The TV was at an angle on a dresser and a potted plant next to it needed watering. There were the remnants of a late-night snack on the coffee table.

"I would have tidied, if I'd known you were coming." The mess was suddenly embarrassing.

"That doesn't concern me. It's you I wanted to see."

She held his gaze. Damn his eyes, they made her want to throw everything away. But she couldn't. She had to stay strong.

"Four things," he said. "For you, from me." He moved to the table and took out two chrome keys. He set them down.

"What are they for?" she asked.

"I'll tell you in a minute." He reached into his pocket again and pulled out a small black velvet box. He placed it next to the keys.

"What's that?"

He didn't answer. Instead, he withdrew a slim collar from his pocket—the one she'd worn during their sex sessions—and added that to the collection of objects on the table.

Seeing the collar sent waves of arousal through Imogen. He had it with him? Her nipples tightened and she pressed her folded arms against them. Did that mean he intended to...? Would she? One last time?

"As you know, I think very highly of you, Imogen, very

highly indeed."

Very highly! What did that mean? Was it his way of saying he loved her? Had she dreamed that he'd spoken those words on their last night together?

"And how we ended things was very unacceptable to me," he said, "so I have put processes in place to try to come to a mutual agreement."

"Okay."

"Issues that concerned you have been alleviated to a significant extent, and I hope you can agree to the new deal."

"You make me sound like a business transaction."

"Oh, no, you're much more important than that."

Imogen said nothing. She waited for him to continue.

"It seemed to me," he said, "that you had three main issues with us being a couple, officially."

"Three?"

"Yes." He nodded. "And I've addressed each in a manner I hope you will find satisfactory so that we can go back to how we both felt on top of the Empire State Building." He paused. "Back then I thought we'd committed to making a go of it, but it seemed my idea of that was very different to yours."

"I think that sums up that conversation, and—"

"You don't want to give up your job," he said in a forceful voice, causing her to pause, "and I understand that. I wouldn't want to give up mine. So I've purchased floors fifty-six and fifty-seven of The Shard—it will be the new home of Ward Enterprises. My new base, somewhere to run operations on a daily basis."

"I don't understand." What the hell was he talking about?

"Until now my staff and I have been spread out globally. I'm bringing us all together, in one place." He paused. "London."

"Here?"

"Yes, here, where you are, Imogen."

"But you can't do that for me."

"I can and I have." He shrugged. "I've also promoted some of my most senior staff—they'll be taking a much more hands-on role and making major decisions, freeing me up from traveling so frequently. I'm hoping to be in London for at least two weeks out of every month."

"Kane, I…" He'd made such massive changes. For her? She couldn't be responsible for that.

"No, wait. I haven't finished."

Her head was full of questions, but it was clear he needed to speak. She pressed her palm over her lips as a way of keeping those words inside.

"This key," he said, holding up the slimmer of the two that he'd placed on the table. "Is to my new home, 134 Billington Road, Kensington."

"Very desirable address."

"So I'm told." He reached for her hand, the one by her mouth, and unfurled her fingers. "And this is *your* key." He set it in her palm. "I wish you to come and go as you please, or perhaps that might change to *as I please*, but that's up for negotiation."

"My key?"

"My home is your home. Much as I like yours"—he glanced about the small space—"I'd like you at my home when I'm there, which will be as often as I can be."

"You're giving me a key, to your house?"

"Of course." He nodded. "How else will you get through the door?"

His expression was stern but Imogen knew him well enough to know he was anxious beneath it. He was asking a lot—would she give it?

"And the other key?" she asked, indicating the one with a black rubber tip.

"Yes." He picked it up. "This actually won't be in your possession but it is yours. I have you a car with a driver that is entirely at your disposal. Whenever you want to come to me, he will bring you. Wherever you want to go, in fact, he will take you."

"A Bentley?"

He paused. A flicker of confusion flashed over his eyes, then he nodded as if connecting the dots. "Yes. A Bentley."

So that was the purchase she'd seen on his accounts. It had cost several hundred thousand pounds for the car alone, before the driver's wages. "It's too much."

"What? To have you come to my home whenever you want? It's a small price and it's done now." He shrugged. "I don't want you to be too tired to face evening traffic to drive to Kensington after a day at the bank. I want you at my home if I'm there."

"You already said that."

"And do you agree?"

She could feel herself softening. He'd put a lot of thought and effort, not to mention money, into solving their dilemma. *Their* dilemma. That was the point, he was coming to the halfway mark, overstepping it, in fact. He'd reached out.

"Damn it," he said, shaking his head and biting his bottom lip. "I really should have got another helicopter; that would have made the most sense. There is room for a helipad on the roof and I'm sure we could have arranged something at Coutts…"

"No, no…" She stepped up to him. "The car is fine, a helicopter is overkill." She rested her hand on his arm. "Besides, I can share yours."

"Everything I have is yours." His voice was lower. "Imogen, I know I'm a workaholic, and a mess when it comes to relationships. But—"

"Whoa… why are you a mess?"

He sighed and glanced away. "The only other woman who I've… had strong feelings for left me. I couldn't give her my time. She asked for nothing else. Much like you, she just wanted to be with me. I let her go because I was busy and I won't say I don't regret that, I do. But it's ancient history. What I don't want to do is let it happen again.

You've got inside." He paused and patted his chest, the black shirt pressed against his wide pecs. "Here."

And he'd certainly got inside her chest. She stared at his wide fingers and neat nails. She was glad his previous relationship hadn't worked out because it meant he was available for her. And it sounded like the pain had made him determined not to repeat his mistake.

Right now she didn't want to make the mistake of not seeing what he'd done. He'd gone to the midpoint and now she needed to meet him there. And it was doable; he'd listened to her and had made it so.

Oh, she loved him for that. So damn much. Every part of him.

She placed her hand over his. "I'm glad you're going to be in London more."

"And we can spend time together?"

She held up the key. "Yes." Was this really happening? "I'd like that, a lot."

"You'll come to Kensington?"

"It's an offer I can't refuse." She smiled—a big wide smile that stretched her lips, bunched her cheeks, and went right up to her eyes. "You've really done that? You really are going to be based in London?"

"I need to be where you are, not where the CEOs of every other global conglomerate is."

"I… Kane… I've missed you so much."

"And I you." He grabbed her and dragged her up against his body. "It was a crazy whirlwind of lust in New York, but…" His lips stretched downward, his eyes screwed up. He looked in pain.

"What?"

"I need you." He'd blurted the words out.

"I need you too." She wrapped her hands around the nape of his neck and pulled him close; the key fell to the floor. She pressed her lips to his, darted her tongue out, and kissed him in a way that she hoped told him she loved him. Even more so now that he'd worked out how they could be together without her having to give up her life.

She controlled the kiss for all of two seconds, then he took over; he tilted his head, deepened his tongue, and dragged her closer.

After a few minutes she broke the kiss. "You said there were four things."

His lips were shiny, his eyes flashed. "Yes." He released her and stepped back.

For a moment he was still, as though composing himself. He smoothed his shirt then ran a hand over his hair.

Imogen watched. Her heart was thumping.

"This," he said, raising the collar into the air, "has to be part of us."

"I always thought it would be."

"And how much of a problem is that?"

She thought for a moment, memories rushing through her mind. "I enjoyed what we did. You saw that for yourself. How could you not?"

"And you said that you were willing to build on it."

"Yes." She hesitated. "I'm not ready for Marie's situation, though. To obey without question all day, every day."

"I get that. I won't push it." He shook his head and slid the collar through his fingers. "It just makes me feel complete, in touch with myself to have you submit. To know that you trust me so much, that you're mine, totally, absolutely." He pressed the buckle to his lips, kissed it, and his eyes fluttered shut. "But it's just you now. I'm not interested in any other sub. This dark corner of my desires only wants you to enter the shadows."

"Are you sure?"

"How can you even question that?" He opened his eyes wide and stared at her.

"I don't know what you've been doing while we've been apart, Kane. You're a master dom, you could have been doing many different things with many different people."

"I could say the same about you." He released the collar

so it hung from his fingers.

"I haven't... I've missed you too much. I couldn't even think about..."

"So we're on the same page. No one else."

"No one else."

"And you'll wear my collar?"

"When we're..."

"In the bedroom or in a scene. You said that already."

"Yes."

"And one day more?" He looked hopeful, his brow creased as he worried at his bottom lip with his teeth.

What would happen if she said no?

She didn't want to say no.

"I'm not sure. Perhaps." She stared at the loop of leather. "You'll have to guide me to a place where I understand and feel comfortable with that situation."

"I can. I will."

"Then that particular clause is open and still up for negotiation."

He sucked in a breath and blew it out through pursed lips.

"Can you live with that?" she asked.

"Yes, I can."

She looked at the table. There was one thing left on it—the small black velvet box.

"What's that?"

He picked it up. "If you wear my collar." He stepped up to her, close, then dropped to his knees. "Then I also want you to wear this. But not just in the bedroom. At all times, as a way to let the world know that there is a man who loves and treasures you more than anything else he owns."

"Kane." A sob grew in her chest and burst upward. Was it really what she thought it might be? She hadn't dared hope. Wouldn't let herself believe they were at that point.

"Imogen." He opened the lid, revealing a stunning diamond ring. The light caught off the glittering edges, sending sparkles around the rim of the case. "Marry me."

"I…"

"Marry me, be mine, be everything you can be and let's see what else we can achieve together." He took her hand, kissed her knuckles. "Let's share our lives and make it work on every level. Allow our bodies, minds, and souls to be as one."

"I don't know what to say."

"Say yes." He gripped her hand. "Because I'm never going to say goodbye to you. I can't."

"In that case… yes."

He gritted his teeth and shut his eyes. He leaned forward, wrapping his arms around her hips and burying his face against her stomach.

She clutched his head, holding him close.

Her big strong man was on his knees at her feet. He'd never been more adorable or perfect than in that moment.

"Yes," she said again, dragging her hands through his hair. "I will marry you."

He stared up at her, his features tight with emotion. "I'll make you so happy," he said. "I promise."

"I know. I know you will." She pulled at his shirt, urging him to stand. "You don't have to do anything except be here and I'll be happy."

"I will be. What I've been doing all these years has been a means to an end. It took me a while to understand what it was all for, what that end is, but now I know."

"What?" She stroked his cheek.

"I want you to be happy, I want…" He glanced away.

"Tell me, please."

He didn't look at her. Instead, he took her left hand and slipped the ring onto her finger. It fit perfectly. "I've purchased a plot of land in Kent."

She knew that already but had no idea why he'd bought it.

"I intend to build us a country retreat. A place to get away from it all at weekends… a place for children to have ponies, ride bikes, build treehouses, do you know what I mean?"

She smiled. She did know what he meant and it was real. All of it. They were going to be together, not just for a few wild nights in New York but long term. She studied the ring—it was predictably huge and beautiful. But at the moment it could have been cheap plastic from a Christmas cracker and she would have been the happiest woman on Earth.

"What do you think of that plan?" Kane asked, lifting his gaze from her hand. "Kent?"

"I think it sounds wonderful. A perfect plan for the future."

He didn't smile, but his eyes told her he was as happy as she was. He tugged her near and kissed her, hard.

She clung to him, pressed close but couldn't get close enough. His tongue tangled with hers, their noses touched, and his breaths were hard on her cheek.

"Where the hell is your bedroom?" he asked.

"Through there." She nodded to her left.

"Will you?" He held up the collar.

"I…"

"Nothing kinky. I've told you before, sometimes vanilla is the best flavor, but…"

"But you like me to wear it."

He nodded, once.

She scooped her hair up, exposing her neck, and allowed her fiancé to carefully secure the collar.

"Perfect," he said as she released her hair. "You're so beautiful."

"So take me to bed and show me how beautiful I am." Her stomach was in knots, her body aching for his touch.

"I'm the one who gives instructions, remember." A brief smile crossed his lips before he swept her up and kissed her.

He moved quickly to the bedroom, pushed open the door to the darkness, and somehow found the bed. He rested her on it, pressing himself over her and spreading kisses over her cheek, to her ear, then down her throat.

She yanked at his shirt, freeing it from the waistband of his trousers.

He slipped his hands beneath her cotton sweater and cupped her breasts. "I was so scared I'd never touch you again," he murmured onto her cheek.

"I felt the same. I've been so miserable."

He paused and lifted her top off, released her bra. "Me too, though being busy helped." He squashed her breasts together and licked through her cleavage before swirling his tongue around her nipples. "But I could still taste you, when I remembered that night on the cross. Your taste was in my memory."

She yanked harder at his shirt and he allowed her to remove it.

Skin on skin, that's what she needed; she wriggled beneath him, ensuring maximum contact.

He slipped lower, hooked his fingers beneath her sweats and tugged them off, dragging her knickers with them. He tossed the bundle of material aside, then sat between her spread legs.

Imogen stared up at him through the shadows. Any vulnerability in him had gone—now he reminded her of a hunter who'd caught his prey. She was breathing fast, her breasts shifting with each lungful of air.

He placed his hands on her inner thighs, parted her legs until her hips had a sweet stretch in the joints, then pressed his face to her pussy.

"Oh... oh..." Imogen gasped, reaching behind her head for the slatted headboard and gripping it. He wasn't teasing or taking it slowly. He'd taken her clit into his mouth and pushed two, maybe three fingers into her entrance.

She shoved her heels into the mattress and arched her spine. He was building her up so fast—weeks of half-hearted masturbation had left her wanting and needy. He didn't let up. If anything, his determination to make her come increased.

"Oh... Kane... I'm going to..." Fuck, if he didn't want

her to orgasm on his face, he should stop now.

He lifted up, grabbed her left leg, and twisted her lower body so her left buttock was exposed. "Come."

A sudden sharp pain rang over her flesh, heating it instantly and blooming to her swollen, sensitive clit.

"Ow... ow... ah..." she cried, squeezing the wood with more force as the smack itself threatened to tip her into climax.

He gripped her buttocks and lifted her pussy to his face. He shoved his tongue into her and his nose bashed her clit. In and out his firm tongue went, fucking her.

She ground onto him and allowed her orgasm to spill over. She cried out as release ravaged her body. Wetness burst from her and he lapped it up, taking all of her.

Her pussy spasmed against his tongue and her skin tingled all over.

"So fucking beautiful," he said, raising his head and slipping his fingers into her. "That's it, hold onto this."

"Oh... God... yes..." She curled to the side as he stroked over her G-spot. The sensations were so dense and she was still throbbing through her climax. A long, low moan rumbled up from her chest; she hardly noticed it was her making the noise.

He massaged and rubbed, expertly easing her through the final stages.

Eventually, she dragged in a breath and opened her eyes. "Kane." Seeing him between her legs, studying her pussy, fingers lodged high, was nearly enough to spark the climb to another orgasm.

"So responsive," he murmured.

"I am when you do that."

He looked up. He smiled as if seeing her spread out, wanton, sweaty, and sated pleased him very much.

"How about when I do this." He stood, quickly removed the rest of his clothing, then climbed over her.

His body weight was delicious, and when the tip of his cock nudged her mound she spread her legs, reached down, and guided him to her entrance.

"I've missed your hands on me," he said.

"I don't think I've had my hands on you that much. Every other part of me, but not hands."

He pushed in an inch. "We'll have to rectify that."

She released him and gripped his buttocks. "Yes."

"But later," he said, his voice tense, "that will have to be later, because right now... I just need..." He forged in, full depth.

Imogen grunted as his chest pushed against hers and he filled her completely.

"That's where... I wanted to be..." he said, propping onto one elbow and smoothing her hair from her forehead with his free hand.

She squeezed his ass. "Yes..."

"I want all of you."

"You have all of me."

"Have you been using the plug?"

She shook her head. "No... I didn't see—"

"The point. That's okay." He slipped halfway out then rocked back in, catching her clit on his wiry pubic hair and hard body. "We'll start again with that. We have all the time in the world now... for everything." He caught her mouth in a slow, deep kiss.

Imogen raised her pelvis to meet his gentle thrusts. She knew she'd come again, it was hovering right there. For several minutes she let it tease her, play with her. She was enjoying being close to Kane, as close as two people could be.

"I can't hold off," he said. "I'm going to come, in you... now." He slipped his hand over her neck, not tight, just resting over the collar.

She dug her nails into his flesh, wrapped her legs around his thighs, and as he gave several more forceful thrusts she allowed another climax to ravish her.

His gasps of ecstasy blasted into her ear as she came. Her pussy clenched his steely cock, and her breasts butted his chest, his body hair scratching her nipples.

"Fuck, fuck…" he moaned, curling his hips under a final time.

A tremor traveled down his spine and she held him closer as though keeping him together.

"So damn good to feel you come on my dick," he said, raising his head and staring down at her, his hand still at her throat. "And I'm not leaving it so long before I fuck you again."

She smiled. "Glad to hear it, Sir."

He groaned as if the word itself were physical stimulation. "You're going to be the most satisfied, desired, contented woman to ever walk on this planet; you do know that, don't you?"

"I can live with that." She gave a breathless giggle, and he removed his fingers from the collar.

He kissed her, then slipped out and flopped onto the bed. He scooped her close.

Imogen clung to his upper arms as they wrapped around her. Her new ring caught a shard of light and sparkled. "What about the clubs?" she said, kissing his nipple.

"What do you mean?" He wound his legs with hers.

"Are you still going ahead with them?" She had wondered if it had all been an elaborate plan to get her to visit one.

"Of course. The one in London is being assessed by architects as we speak. Soon conversion and building work will take place and then the final interior details."

"And the others? In Berlin and Rome?"

"I've purchased the properties, just working out contracts with local authorities." He ran a finger down her spine then rested his hand over her buttock—the one that still held heat from her one spank.

"And do you really need my help with designing or was that all a ploy?"

"Of course I still want your help." He sounded surprised that she'd think otherwise. "After all, the one in London is going to be somewhere we can play too." He hesitated. "If you'd like that."

She looked up at him. Their own club to play in? Somewhere lust, love, pleasure, pain, and kink would have room to breathe, be expressed—be indulged in. She couldn't think of anything more fun, not when she had her very own master of the game to show her the way and teach her the rules.

"I'd like that very much," she said.

"Imogen..." He shook his head, frowned. "Have you any idea how much I love you?"

His words settled in her chest. Her eyes pricked. "I love you too, Kane Ward." She kissed him.

He ran his fingers into her hair and held her head. "I love you so much, more than you can ever imagine."

"Then show me... again."

Suddenly she was on her back and he was over her. "You should get a spank for giving me orders," he said, his cock thickening against her thigh.

"Okay..." she said, a smile twisting her lips.

"Oh, you're going to be so much fun."

He slid into her and Imogen gripped his shoulders. She'd started her day sad, alone, and broken-hearted, but now all of her dreams had come true. The man she loved was in her bed, her arms, in her, and they had so much to look forward to. The future offered dark delights and sweet treats, and it was all going to be delicious.

# EPILOGUE

*Two weeks later…*

*LONDON DAILY NEWS*
*The London Daily News is delighted to exclusively announce the engagement of British tycoon Kane Ward to Coutts' bank manager Imogen White.*

*In a rare interview, Kane Ward stated that "I've never been happier and my new fiancée has made my world complete."*

*With a Caribbean wedding set to take place over Christmas, no expense will be spared as this most secretive of billionaires finally ties the knot.*

*But the blushing bride is not only busy planning the big day, she's also just been appointed to the board of directors at Coutts Bank. Imogen White is the first female to take up the position at this prestigious company, and the official statement is "Ms. White is forward thinking, strong, and an asset to the board. Her dedication and commitment made her the perfect choice for the role. We are lucky to have her."*

*London Daily News would like to congratulate the happy couple and wish them many blissful years together.*

# THE END

Made in the USA
Monee, IL
12 November 2021